Apache Mountain Justice

RAY HOGAN

Sagebrush
Large Print Westerns

Library of Congress Cataloging in Publication Data

Hogan, Ray, 1908-
    Apache Mountain justice / Ray Hogan.
        p. (large print)   cm.
    ISBN 1-57490-112-5 (alk. paper)
    1. Large type books.   I. Title.
[PS3558.O3473A88   1997]
813'.52—dc21   96-52576
                                                                                CIP

Cataloguing in Publication Data is available from
the British Library and the National Library of Australia.

Sagebrush Large Print Westerns are published in the United States
and Canada by Thomas T. Beeler, Publisher, Box 659, Hampton
Falls, New Hampshire 03844-0659. ISBN 1-57490-112-5

Published in the United Kingdom, Eire, and the Republic of South
Africa by Isis Publishing Ltd, 7 Centremead, Osney Mead, Oxford
OX2 0ES England. ISBN 0-7531-5543-5

Published in Australia and New Zealand by Australian Large Print
Audio & Video Pty Ltd, 17 Mohr Street, Tullamarine, Victoria, 3043,
Australia. ISBN 1-86340-694-8   JUL 2 4 1997

Manufactured in the United States of America

CHAPTER 1

FRANK BRATTON STIFFENED, BUT THE STOLID expression on his hard-cut features did not change. Madden, the gambler sitting to his left, had once again slipped a card from the sleeve of his coat into the palm of his hand. It was a cheap, two-bit cardsharp trick that Bratton had not expected to encounter in a gambling house like Charlie's Place, one so well known and highly thought of along the border.

Settling back in his chair, Bratton glanced at the two other players at the table. The one to his immediate right had been introduced as Prentice Axtel by Charlie Thorne, the owner of the casino. Friends called him "Print" Axtel, a short, heavyset, balding man, Frank had informed him. Axtel was in the hay and grain business in nearby El Paso. Next to him was Amos Slaughter, a red-faced, tobacco-chewing cattleman who had a ranch over in the Gila country some miles to the west. A slow thinker, Slaughter was also a poor poker player.

Jace Madden was something else. Apparently making his headquarters at Thorne's, he was a slim, well-dressed man with sly, deliberate ways and dark, shuttered eyes that seemed to take in everything. Evidently neither Axtel nor Slaughter had noticed Madden's crooked move but Thorne, standing just to one side of the gambler, should have. Frank raised a questioning look at him, but Thorne was staring off across the deserted room to the bar where a woman, probably his wife, was washing glasses behind the short counter.

Charlie's Place was not a saloon in the usual sense of

1

the word. Liquor was available to those who desired it, but the establishment was devoted to high-stakes gambling. Tucked away in that small triangle of the New Mexico territory, wedged between Texas and Mexico, Charlie's Place was well patronized by the card-playing gentry. At the moment, however, only one of its eight tables was in use, since it was just midafternoon.

Bratton continued to study Thorne. If the casino owner had seen Madden's sleeve trick, he had chosen not to show it. Shifting about, Thorne stepped back from his casual, onlooker position beside Madden and drew a leather billfold from an inner pocket of his coat. Fumbling, he dropped and retrieved it hurriedly. Then, shaking his head as if deploring his own clumsiness, he restored it to its place inside his coat.

"You staying or folding?" Jace Madden pressed impatiently, eyes on Amos Slaughter.

The cattleman considered his cards, lifted his eyes to assess the pot, an assortment of coins and currency amounting to nearly a thousand dollars, piled in the center of the table.

"Cost you a hundred dollars . . ."

Slaughter shrugged, counted out five double eagles, and tossed them into the pot.

"I'm in so damn deep now, I reckon I ain't got no choice other'n to stay," he grumbled.

Indifferent, Madden turned his attention to Print Axtel. "You?"

"Too steep for me," the merchant replied gloomily, and threw down his cards. "Way my luck's been running, I couldn't win with four aces."

Madden glanced at Frank. Outside the low, rambling building a horse and rider raced by at a fast gallop, apparently headed for the town—one saloon, a general store, a stable, and a hotel—a quarter of a mile or so on to the west. The settlement had no name, and was generally referred to as that "honky-tonk town" near Charlie's Place.

"Up to you, friend," Madden said. "Either you're in or you ain't."

Bratton shook his head. "Don't call me friend," he said in a flat voice, and added, "I'm in if you'll throw away that card you got out of your sleeve and use the one that's on the floor."

Abruptly the room was filled with tension. Slaughter and Axtel came to attention while Thorne drew back another step from Madden. At the bar the woman had paused at her chores and was watching the men closely.

"You accusing me of cheating?" the gambler demanded in a low, tight voice.

"Twice saw you skin a card out of your sleeve," Bratton replied. "That's cheating far as I'm concerned."

The corners of Jace Madden's jaw whitened, and his eyes narrowed. At once Thorne moved up to stand beside Bratton.

"You're making a hell of a mistake," he said to Bratton. "Jace has been running a table here at my place for better'n a year, and I ain't never had no complaints."

Bratton's wide shoulders stirred. In his mid-twenties, he was a tall, muscular man with dark eyes and hair and a firm jaw. Dressed in ordinary range clothing, he looked more like a cowhand cleaned up for Saturday night than the professional gambler he was. Not long ago he had been on the wrong side of the law, but through fate and a twist of luck, he had discovered he could make more money with less danger at the poker tables.

3

"Maybe so, Charlie, but you saw him pull it, unless you've all of a sudden gone blind. You were standing right there beside him."

"Never seen nothing," Thorne declared flatly.

Bratton swore deeply. "Card'll be right there on the floor. Could be a couple of them. Axtel, take a look."

"No, by God!" Madden shouted, whirling half around.

As he turned, his right hand made a stab for the weapon he carried. Bratton was alert for any such move and reacted swiftly, drawing his own gun. Swinging it fast and hard, he clubbed the gambler alongside the head. There was a dull, meaty thud as the heavy .45 laid its mark on Madden's temple. The gambler slumped to one side, slid limply from his chair, and sprawled onto the floor.

Bratton sprang to his feet and glanced around. Both Axtel and Slaughter had risen also, and Thorne, jaw sagging, moved quickly in to kneel beside Madden. After a few moments he drew himself upright.

"Dead—you've gone and killed Jace!"

Bratton shook his head in disbelief. He bent over to make his own examination. A steadily darkening blue welt along the gambler's temple told him where the blow had landed. Charlie Thorne was right; there was no doubt that Madden was dead. Frank glanced at the three men.

"Didn't aim to kill him. Just wanted to keep him from using his gun on me."

"Well, he's dead," Thorne stated, looking toward the bar. "And there weren't no cause for you to do it."

Bratton's eyes narrowed. "There was plenty. He was a cardsharp. I caught him sleeve-dealing and called his hand on it. He went for his gun, and I stopped him."

4

"Was you calling him a cheat that made him go for his gun," Thorne said, again turning his eyes toward the bar. The woman was gone. "What you done was murder."

"Madden was a crook and I'm getting a hunch you knew that," Bratton said in a low, even tone.

"You're mighty handy at calling folks hard names," Thorne said. "You ain't got proof of anything you've claimed."

"I know what I saw," Frank shot back, and motioned to Amos Slaughter. "Start splitting that pot up—three ways. Axtel, you take that look under Madden's chair—maybe under him now. Cards will be down there somewhere."

Axtel circled the table and, pushing chairs aside, began to search around. Bratton waited, idly watching the cattleman divide the cash into three equal amounts—the customary procedure when a game ended as theirs had. Thorne looked on coldly.

"Ain't no cards down here nowheres," Axtel announced after a few moments of pushing furniture aside to let light from the lamp chandelier overhead illuminate the area. Pulling himself erect, he faced Bratton. "You sure you seen Madden throw away them cards?"

"No, never said that. Said I saw him draw one out of his sleeve for certain, and maybe two. He would've dropped the cards he didn't want so's the count in his hand would be right."

"Well, there sure ain't no cards on the floor."

Bratton began to rake in the currency and coins Slaughter had shoved toward him. He looked up at Thorne. "I reckon you can explain what happened to them, can't you, Charlie?" He remembered that Thorne

5

had let his billfold fall to the floor near Madden's feet and had hastily retrieved it.

"I ain't got nothing to explain. You're just trying to cover up killing a man."

Bratton shifted his gaze to Slaughter as he pointed to his share of the pot. "What's the count?"

"Right close to three hundred."

Bratton separated thirty dollars from his third of the money and tossed it back onto the table. "There's your ten percent," he said to Thorne. "Far as me killing Madden, it was an accident, and it was in self-defense. You know that. He was cheating and he—"

"No proof he was cheating," Print Axtel said. "Leastwise, we ain't seen any."

"Count the cards he was holding," Bratton directed, impatient. "Maybe he didn't drop them like I figured."

Thorne stepped forward and started to pick up the hand Jace Madden had held. Bratton waved him off with the gun he still held in his hand. Bucking his head at Slaughter, he said, "You do it."

The cattleman took up the cards and counted them off one at a time. "Ain't but five. Three aces, a deuce, and a six," he said.

Thorne laughed. "I reckon that proves what's what. Jace was playing square."

"Only proves that something happened to those cards," Bratton said, anger tightening his features. "And you know what it was."

"Now, how the hell could I—"

"I recollect you dropped your billfold right after I saw Madden slip a card out of his sleeve. You let it fall close to where Madden was sitting and then you picked up both the card and the billfold right quick." Frank paused, turned to Axtel and Amos Slaughter. "Didn't

6

either one of you see that?"

The feed merchant shrugged. "Was playing cards. Wasn't thinking about nothing else."

"Same here," Slaughter said. "When a man's got a powerful lot of his money sunk in a game, he ain't bothering about nothing else 'cepting what's in his hand."

A smile was on Charlie Thorne's lips. "I'd say you've got yourself in a picklement, mister. You was losing big to Jace, so you trumped up this here card thing you claim he pulled. Then when he called you a liar, you egged him into going for his gun and killed him."

"That was an accident, you all know that. And he was reaching for—"

A voice from the doorway interrupted their bickering. "What's the trouble here?"

CHAPTER 2

BRATTON TURNED HIS ATTENTION TO THE GAMBLING house entrance. A crooked smile pulled at his lips as he recognized the man in the doorway. To the left of Bratton, Charlie Thorne took it upon himself to reply to the newcomer's question.

"Been a killing, Marshal. Fellow here—don't know his name up and clubbed—"

"I know him. Name's Frank Bratton," the lawman said, moving farther into the room. Halting at the edge of the half-circle formed by the four men, he nodded curtly to Frank. "Figured I'd be running into you again. Ain't hardly been a year since you got let out, has it?"

"Little more," Bratton said coolly. "Before you go making up your mind, do you want to hear my side of

7

this?"

"We ain't doing nothing till you hand that gun over to me."

Bratton stepped forward, passed his weapon butt first to the federal marshal, and then, dropping back, folded his arms across his chest and waited. The lawman, U.S. Deputy Marshal Harry Locke, was no stranger to him. Hard and relentless, Locke was a man of towering pride who had a reputation for sticking religiously to the letter of the law.

"You know this drifter?" Charlie Thorne asked.

"Reckon I do. He's been in the pen a couple of times—know that much," Locke replied, moving around to where he could have a look at the sprawled figure of the dead gambler. "Who's the stiff one?"

"Name's Jace Madden. Ran a table here in my place," Charlie said. "Good man. Honest."

"Well, he's done filling in straights now," the marshal drawled as he came back around to face the others.

Harry Locke had changed little since he last saw him in San Antonio, Bratton noted. Well into his fifties, he was a short, lean man with a full mustache, squinting, dark eyes, and heavy brows. He was dressed as Frank remembered him—longsleeved gray shirt; red neckerchief, black leather vest, to which he pinned his star; brown corduroy pants; knee-high boots, scuffed and worn from considerable service; and a weathered, shapeless gray hat. He carried his bone-handled .45 Colt six-gun well forward on his right thigh, just as always.

"Then I expect you know what this Bratton is. A gunman, a killer," Charlie Thorne began. "We—"

"I don't know no such a damn thing," Locke said calmly. "Bratton, you want to tell me what happened?"

Frank shrugged. "Madden, there, was a cardsharp. I

8

caught him at it. He went for his gun and—"

"And you beat him to the trigger. Seems I've heard that from you before."

"Didn't shoot him. I hit him alongside the head with my gun. Wallop shouldn't've killed him, but it did."

"Jace wasn't doing no cheating, Marshal," Thorne said. "We proved that."

Locke frowned, clawed at the stubble of beard on his chin. He had evidently been on the trail for several days and had not had the opportunity to shave. He shifted his gaze to Bratton.

"That so?"

"No. Saw Madden deal himself a card out of his coat sleeve. Twice, I think, and once for sure."

"Won't be hard to find out if that's true," Locke said. "Count the deck."

"I figure he dropped the card he didn't want to the floor—"

"Weren't none on the floor, Marshal. I looked real good," Axtel volunteered.

Locke considered the merchant narrowly. "Who're you?"

"Name's Prentice Axtel. Run a feed store over in El Paso."

"And you?" the lawman continued, glancing at Slaughter.

"Amos Slaughter. Own a ranch west of here."

"You two the only other men sitting in the game?"

"We were," the cattleman replied, and spat a stream of tobacco juice at a nearby cuspidor.

Thorne's woman was again behind the bar. Undoubtedly she had been the one to summon the marshal, who was probably just passing through the settlement, Bratton guessed. He felt Locke's small eyes

9

drilling into him.

"What've you got to say about this here Axtel claiming there weren't no cards on the floor?"

Frank's shoulders stirred. "Either Thorne picked them up or kicked them out of the way."

Thorne swore angrily and took a step toward Bratton. Harry Locke waved him aside and picked up the cards.

"Reckon I'll just count the deck like I said," he remarked, and began going through the deck. When he was finished, he tossed the cards back onto the table and turned to Bratton.

"Fifty-two," he stated, his manner hardening. "I'm starting to wonder if maybe these people ain't right—that you didn't have no call to kill the gambler. You know Madden from somewheres?"

"Never heard of him till I came here looking for a game."

"That's mighty hard to believe," Thorne said. "He plain ragged Jace into going for his gun. I figure he was carrying a grudge."

"Yeah, maybe Madden cleaned him out in a game somewheres," Axtel suggested, "and he come here looking to get even."

"Could be," the marshal agreed mildly, his attention still on Bratton. "What was that you was saying about Thorne picking up the cards you claim Madden dropped, or maybe kicking them out of sight? That just you scrambling, trying to worm out of this?"

"No, he stood alongside Madden most of the time while we were playing. Once he dropped his billfold, then picked it up right quick. And he done a lot of shuffling around. Could have been dragging a card out from under Madden's chair."

Locke transferred his gaze to the casino owner. "I

10

sure would like to hear your answer to that."

Thorne drew a cigar from an inner pocket and bit off the closed end. Ridding himself of the bit of leaf, he fired a match with a thumbnail. Holding the flame to the tip of the brown cylinder, he puffed it into life.

"Oh, hell, Marshal!" he said in obvious disgust. "You didn't just come in on a load of turnips! Anybody can see Bratton's saying that to keep from getting hung for killing Jace." Thorne hesitated, then shook his head. "Why would I be doing something like he claims? This here's my place. I don't need to—"

"Could be you and Madden were working together, splitting his winnings," Frank said, cutting in.

Harry Locke gave that thought as he rubbed at his chin. Turning once more to Bratton, he said, "When it comes down to rock bottom, you saying you never seen Thorne pick up any cards? You figure only that maybe he did?"

Bratton smiled wearily. He had already stated that he had not actually seen Charlie Thorne retrieve the cards the gambler had thrown away. To change that and say he did would be a lie—one Harry Locke would sense immediately. And that's just what the lawman wanted. It would settle this little matter quickly—there'd be no doubt that Frank was guilty. Best he continue to be truthful. The marshal would respect that, and undoubtedly decide that his actions had been justifiable. Then he would forget the whole thing.

"No, can't say that I did, but from the way he stayed around Madden, I'd say that's where the cards went," Frank responded.

"Which sure'n hell ain't so!" Charlie said, shaking his head vigorously. "I run an honest game. Ain't never let no tinhorns and cardsharps work my tables if I knew

11

about it."

"He's telling you the truth, Marshal," Axtel said. "I've been coming over here off and on for about a year, and I ain't never run into a crooked game."

Locke's thin lips parted in a smile. "Sometimes a man don't know when he's getting skinned—"

Axtel flushed. "Maybe so, but I sure would. Expect I'd know in a minute if I was getting fleeced."

"Yeah, I reckon you would," the lawman agreed, and nodded to Thorne. "There somebody around here that can take care of the stiff, or you want to send—"

"I'll see to it," Thorne said quickly. I've got a couple of swampers that can handle it." His features clouded with concern. "You ain't turning Bratton loose, are you?"

"No, I'm taking him in. Going to let a judge decide what's what. You all claim he egged this Madden into drawing on him over nothing—"

"Why the hell would I want to do that?" Bratton demanded, suddenly angry. He had depended on Harry Locke for a fair shake, but it looked now as if he weren't going to get one. And being locked up in a jail again after all the time he'd spent in prison was the last thing he wanted. His confidence in the lawman's fairness was steadily diminishing. "Told you I caught him cheating—"

"Now, your saying that plain don't make it so," Locke drawled. "All comes down to this—we've got a dead man and he was killed by you. Got three witnesses right on the spot saying you done it for no reason, and you can't prove otherwise. Means a judge'll have to take care of it."

"I had a reason," Frank repeated doggedly. "Madden was a crook—"

"Only thing I can do is lock you up till a judge comes along to listen to the facts. Meanwhile I'll try to sort things out, do some asking around about this Jace Madden." The lawman paused, glanced at Thorne. "Be asking about you too. See exactly what kind of a joint you're running here."

"Just help yourself. Do all the asking around you're of a mind to. I ain't got nothing to hide," Thorne said, and then added, "Where you aim to lock up Bratton? There ain't no place in the settlement."

"Taking him to El Paso. Have to borrow Dallas Stoudenmeyer's jail till I can get him to the Turkey Springs lockup forty miles from here."

"Why'll you have to do that?" Print Axtel wanted to know. "The jail in El Paso's said to be one of the finest in the country."

"I know that, but the killing took place in New Mexico territory. Means he'll have to be tried before a New Mexico judge, and the nearest one'll be in Turkey Springs."

"Was it me that had the say-so, I'd be for taking care of him right here and now," Amos Slaughter declared, splattering the cuspidor with a stream of amber juice. "Far as I'm concerned, a killer's got the same treatment coming to him that we give to rustlers."

"Maybe you ought to be a judge," Locke said dryly, and turned to Bratton. "Let's go—and you gents, the judge'll likely want to talk to you right along with Thorne there," he added to Axtel and the cattleman.

"Sure thing, Marshal," Thorne said, answering for all three of them. "You know right where to find us."

With Bratton a step in front of him, Locke crossed the dimly lit room and stepped out into the fading day. "My horse is down at the hotel rack. Best we get yours first."

Bratton swore quietly, keeping his anger curbed. "Want you to know you're handing me a raw deal, Locke. I've kept my nose clean ever since I got out of the pen. That cardsharp and Thorne were working together. It ought to be plain to you."

"Could be you're right, but I'm leaving it up to the judge," the lawman said agreeably. "That your horse there at the rack?" he continued as they reached the the livery stable.

Bratton nodded woodenly. The thought of spending endless time once more behind bars weighed heavily on his mind—particularly since he had done nothing to warrant it.

"All saddled up and ready to ride," Harry Locke noted of Bratton's bay gelding, his inference clear. "Now, how's it happen you didn't stable him like any man would've who was aiming to set in on maybe an all-night poker game?"

"Wanted to see how things were in there first," Frank said. "If the looks of the game suited me, then I was going to come back out and—"

"Hold it," the lawman barked suddenly, his attention on two men moving briskly toward them from the direction of the hotel. "They friends of yours?"

"Don't know them," Bratton replied after a moment.

The men drew nearer. Locke swore, hawked, and spat into the dust. "Couple of Texas Rangers—"

Bratton caught the glint of the stars the men were wearing at that moment. He laughed wryly. "Well, they sure'n hell ain't after me!"

The lawman made no answer but remained silent as the two men moved up to him and Bratton and halted.

"You're U.S. Marshal Locke, I take it," the older of the pair said. "I'm Tom Vogel. My partner here's Billy

14

Jay Coleman. We're with the Texas Rangers."

"Howdy," Locke said, and shook hands with both. "Can see you're Rangers and I know Coleman there from a while back."

"He the man who done the killing?" Vogel, all business, continued, pointing at Frank.

The marshal nodded. "This here's him. I'm taking him into El Paso for safekeeping in Stoudenmeyer's jail until I can—"

"Afraid not, Marshal," Vogel broke in. "This is Ranger business. We'll be taking over your prisoner."

CHAPTER 3

THERE WAS A LONG, QUIET MOMENT FILLED ONLY WITH a few faint sounds coming from inside the nearby livery stable and the distant cawing of crows. Finally Harry Locke broke the hush.

"No, I reckon not."

Vogel, a lean, square-jawed, bearded man with light eyes and a thin, straight line for a mouth, stiffened. Like all Rangers he was heavily armed, carrying both a pistol and a repeating-rifle.

"I expect you don't savvy how things are here, Marshal," he said in a patronizing tone. "This is Texas. Us Rangers've been seeing to law and order in these parts for quite a spell."

"Been overdoing your job, then," Locke said. "We're in New Mexico, not Texas."

"The hell!" the other declared hotly.

Young, dressed, and equipped much the same as his partner, Billy Jay Coleman had the impatient, energetic look of a man anxious to make his mark. He started to

15

say more, but Vogel silenced him with a lifted hand as he nodded to the federal marshal.

"I suppose you're right when you get down to the bottom of the bucket, but this strip along here's looked on as just a piece of El Paso—and that means it's in Texas."

"Still don't make it Texas," Locke said. "You've got no authority here."

"The question's come up before," Vogel said, his voice becoming tight as his temper rose, "and I sure ain't of a mind to stand here and jaw about it again."

Bratton leaned against the wall of the stable, a half-smile on his lips. Lawmen arguing about which of them was going to throw him in jail—it was funny except that whoever won out, he was still the loser. His eyes narrowed as the smile faded. Both Rangers and Harry Locke were turned from him as they spoke—and his horse was but a stride or two away. If he could reach the bay gelding, quietly lead him on into the livery barn, he could mount, then leave the stable by the rear door before the lawmen became aware he was gone.

It was a long chance, but it might work. He sure as hell wasn't looking forward to being locked up in the El Paso jail, or any other one. Glancing quickly around to make certain there was no one else around, Frank took a long step toward his horse and stopped. The Rangers and Harry Locke paid him no mind. Sucking in a deep breath, he moved sideways again until he was at the bay's head.

Pausing again, he fiddled casually with the horse's bridle in case one of the lawmen happened to look his way. There was no sign that any of the three was aware of his change in position. The lawmen's voices had become more shrill as the argument progressed, and it

16

looked to Frank as if they'd forgotten him as they disputed jurisdictional rights. Again sucking deep, he jerked the reins free of the hitch rack bar. Ignoring the prickling on the back of his neck, he quickly led the horse into the stable.

As he took the steps Bratton heard one of the Rangers yell. Coleman, he thought. Grim, he vaulted into the saddle and raked his spurs across the flanks of the bay, sending the big horse plunging down the runway for the open doorway he could see at its far end.

Midway, a figure suddenly darted into the runway. A hostler or perhaps the stable's owner. Bratton veered the gelding sharply to avoid running down the startled man and rushed on. A six-gun cracked, filling the barn with echoes. Bratton realized that one of the lawman had fired at him. But the bullet had gone wide, and in the next instant the bay reached the doorway and was pounding out into the open.

The hotel stood immediately west of the livery stable, and as the bay raced toward it, Bratton cut him to the right, then halted. He could hear Locke and the Rangers running hard for their picketed horses. Crouched low, he spurred the gelding into motion. If he could get past the hotel, he could then turn south and make it to the Mexican border—only a mile or so away.

"He'll head for the border!" a voice shouted into the closing day.

Bratton swore as the bay reached the corner of the hotel a low, single-storied adobe structure with a corrugated tin roof and wooden shutters on the windows. The lawmen were actually between him and the border line, an irregular broken stretch of fence, rock, and brush that marked the separation of the two countries. The odds were good that the lawmen would

17

cut him off before he could reach it.

"He won't get far!" Frank recognized the voice of Tom Vogel. "Them Mex *rurales* will nail him the minute he tries to cross over. We made a deal with them a while back."

Bratton swung wide of the hotel and, again spurring the bay, rode hard for a band of tall brush he could see a quarter of a mile or so ahead. He wasted no time in looking to see if Locke and the Rangers had reached their horses and were mounted. Likely they had and were already hurrying to reach the border where they would no doubt split up and ride the line until they encountered him.

The bay, hurrying on through the half-light, had reached the tall brush—a combination of salt cedars, flowering willows, and wild olives—and stopped as Bratton drew him in.

"Expect we'll find the *rurales* holding him right along here somewheres. If one of us runs into him, fire a shot."

It was Vogel and he was nearby. Bratton smiled grimly. The lawmen, having less ground to cover, had gained the dense growth a few minutes ahead of him.

Harry Locke made some sort of reply, but it was unintelligible to Bratton. The marshal was no doubt hopping mad at losing his prisoner and would be blaming the Rangers for it.

"Crusty old bastard, ain't he?"

Vogel was so near that Frank's breath caught in his throat. His hand instinctively dropped to the holster on his hip and fell away. Locke had taken possession of the weapon earlier. Rigid, his hand now moving forward to lie on the bay's taut neck in hope of keeping the horse quiet, Bratton waited out the tense moments in the

18

darkness of the brush. He could hear the two men drawing nearer to join Vogel—the quiet *tunk-tunk* of their horses' hooves, the scrape of leather against a bush, the creak of saddles, and then Vogel's voice once more.

"Let's pull up here and listen a bit. Just might hear that killer going through the brush."

There was silence for several minutes, and then Vogel again spoke. "Heard the marshal say he knew you from somewheres."

"Yeah, up Wichita way. Was four, maybe five years back," Billy Jay responded.

"You get yourself in some kind of trouble?"

"Naw, was nothing much. Happened when I was in the Eagle Saloon. I reckon you remember it."

"Yeah, sure do—"

"Well, me and a couple of friends was at the bar having us a drink when the marshal comes sashaying up and jabs his gun into Billy Joe—he was one of my friends—and says he's under arrest. Was for holding up some counter-jumper down in Waco.

"I was liquored up enough to take it wrong. I grabbed the marshal and jerked him away from Joey. He come halfway around and hit me on the side of the head so hard, I glowed for a week after."

Vogel laughed. "I reckon that taught you not to stick your nose into something that wasn't your business, especially when it's a lawman collaring a fugitive."

"Yeah, it sure did. Sort of like to apologize to him for that, but he's a mite hard to talk to."

"Hell, forget it. Wouldn't mean nothing to him now," Vogel said. "Reckon we better move on. That killer's had time to reach the border and get himself caught by now."

Bratton heard the horses of the two lawmen move off. He waited out a long five minutes, his mind settled on his next move, and when he felt it was safe, he swung the bay around and doubled back toward the settlement.

He'd do what they didn't expect him to. He'd head north. They figured he'd make a run for Mexico where he could be safe from United States law, which was what he had in mind at the start, but that hadn't worked out.

Keeping in the shadows as much as possible, Bratton halted at the edge of the settlement. He would be smart to avoid it completely, not allow anyone to see him. When Harry Locke failed to find him along the border and came back to start over, there would be no trace of him. But to think it would end there was wishful thinking.

Locke was a proud man, one who had boasted often that he'd never lost a prisoner. He was like a bulldog—he'd not quit until he had picked up the trail of his escaped prisoner and finally had him in charge again, thereby preserving his record of invincibility.

He'd feel a hell of a lot better if he had his gun, Bratton thought, moodily studying the settlement now almost enclosed by darkness. But it would be foolhardy to ride in and buy one from the general mercantile; he had to keep in mind that now, after almost a year, he was again an outlaw, a fugitive. Better if he waited until he reached another town. Turkey Springs would be a good bet; it was a day's ride up the river.

Clucking softly to the bay, Bratton rode off along a fringe of brush until he was behind the westernmost building of the settlement, the saloon. A few yards beyond, growth ended, leaving him with a narrow strip of open ground that would have to be crossed before he gained the next stand of cover. Not halting, he rode out into the clear. Too late he saw a man and one of the saloon girls sitting on the landing at the rear of the building.

Cursing his luck, Bratton held the bay to a casual pace, hoping to pass unnoticed or at least to make it appear that he was nothing more than a pilgrim or cowhand on his way to some distant point. About halfway, he slid a covert glance at the couple, anxious to see if they had noticed him. But they were in a close embrace. Bratton's spirits rose again. Maybe luck was with him after all. If it would just hold until he could reach Turkey Springs, he'd have it made.

CHAPTER 4

BRATTON RODE NORTH AT A GOOD PACE FOR TWO miles, then began to angle right until he reached the Rio Grande. There he turned onto a well-beaten road that closely followed the river and pressed on through the creeping darkness.

Harry Locke would not waste much time looking for him along the border, Frank knew. As soon as the marshal realized his prisoner was not in the area, he would double back to Charlie's Place and start asking questions. And if he failed to raise any information of value, he would come to the only logical conclusion— that since the Mexican *rurales* were closely guarding the border, north would be the only route open to his escaped prisoner.

Bratton settled back, trying to brush all thoughts of further trouble, at least for the time being, from his mind. It was pleasant riding along the sluggish, old river

21

in the cool evening hours. Giant, century-old cottonwood trees stood along its banks, their thick-leafed branches silhouetted broadly against the star-flecked sky; coyotes barked from the low hills to either side, and now and then a bird, disturbed by the gelding's passing, chirped sleepily.

A first-quarter moon filled the night with a weak, silvery glow despite its limited size. Several times along the way Bratton saw the low, irregular outlines of small villages huddling in the swales or at the base of a hill.

Bratton would have enjoyed the quiet beauty surrounding him if the threat of Deputy Marshal Harry Locke had not hung, like a dark shadow, in the back of his mind. He shook his head wearily. He had done his level best to keep on the right side of the law for the past year and had been successful at it up to the card game in Charlie's Place. Now that was all changed. To top it off, the lawman who was now trailing him was one of the ironhearted breed from whom he could expect little, if any, understanding.

Bratton had not yet figured out just what he would do. There simply hadn't been time. He had run without thinking. The opportunity for escape to avoid being locked up in El Paso, and later Turkey Springs, had presented itself abruptly, and he had seized it.

Doubtless Harry Locke would have done his best to prove Jace Madden was a tinhorn and that Charlie Thorne was working hand-in-glove with him at the poker tables. The marshal was fair and honest, but his investigations would have taken time—and meanwhile Frank would be sweating it out in a stinking jail cell. Bratton felt he'd already endured all that he intended to. He couldn't leave it to Locke; he would have to go about clearing his name himself—no easy task, since it would be necessary to avoid not only the deputy marshal but other lawmen as well.

He rode on, halting now and then to rest the bay and twice to avoid other pilgrims on the road. He saw three men on horseback and a night stagecoach bound for El Paso. He slept fitfully, dozing off occasionally in the saddle as the bay loped tirelessly on.

Daylight caught him a short distance below Turkey Springs. He halted there on a slight rise, dismounted, and turned his attention to the road behind him. For a good half an hour he studied it and the land to either side while the bay grazed hungrily on a nearby patch of grama grass. Finally convinced that there was no sign of anyone trailing him, Bratton reckoned he had a fair lead over Harry Locke. He mounted and rode on into the town.

A general store at the edge of the settlement offered a place to stock up on trail grub. Heading to the hitch rack, he secured the bay and entered the establishment—erected since his last visit to the town—which bore a sign across its false front that read, JOHNSON'S EMPORIUM.

The store was large and well stocked, and Frank was able to purchase a gun in addition to the necessary food. It was not a new gun, but it was a good secondhand weapon and had a tight cylinder and a soft trigger, much like the .45 Locke had taken from him.

With the comforting and reassuring weight of the gun in the hip holster, Bratton felt much better, and a few minutes later he rode into the main part of Turkey Springs and turned into the first livery stable he saw. Entering the shadowy building, he directed the half-awake hostler to grain, water, and otherwise care for the gelding, making it clear he'd had a long, hard night.

"I'll be back for him in three, maybe four hours. Want him ready to travel again."

"Sure, sure," the hostler muttered, taking the bay's reins. "He'll be ready."

Bratton nodded and turned back to the street, now slowly coming alive with local residents. He wasn't giving the bay much rest, Frank realized, but the gelding was big and strong, and while the ride up from the border had been lengthy, it hadn't been hard. Most likely Frank needed rest more than the bay, but he reckoned he could cure that lack with a couple of stiff drinks and a good meal.

As Frank angled across the wide, dusty street for the Valley Rose, he recalled that it was not only the largest saloon and gambling house between El Paso and Santa Fe, but also one that could provide a man with a decent meal and any other pleasantry he might desire.

He could be taking a chance laying over in Turkey Springs for even a short time, Bratton thought as he mounted the steps to the saloon's ornate batwing doors. But the bay, despite his strength and endurance, still needed a little rest. And since there had been no sign of Harry Locke in that first hour or so of Bratton's escape, it was reasonable to believe the lawman had not taken up the trail north immediately but had continued to search the area around Charlie's Place. Perhaps he had even gone into El Paso, Bratton mused.

The couple at the rear of the saloon near Charlie Thorne's gambling house had probably not noticed him when he rode out. This would also serve as a delay and would keep the marshal off his trail. Whatever happened, Bratton believed he had no choice but to risk the stop for both his and the bay gelding's sakes. He needed the rest—and the time to make plans.

24

Except for two men standing at the bar of the wide, barnlike structure, garishly decorated with banners, paintings, calendars depicting nude women, whiskey advertisements, and other ornaments, the Valley Rose was deserted at that early-morning hour. The bartender, who had probably been on duty all night and was waiting to be relieved, greeted Frank silently with heavy eyes.

"Whiskey," Bratton said. "And I'll be wanting something to eat."

The counterman produced a glass and a bottle of amber liquor. Filling the container to the rim, he pushed it toward Frank. "Two bits."

Bratton produced the required coin and quickly downed the whiskey. "What about the grub?"

"Set yourself down at one of the tables," the bartender replied grumpily. "I'll tell the cook."

Bratton shoved his empty glass at the man, tossing another quarter onto the bar. Taking the drink with him, he moved off toward a darker corner where he would be less noticeable.

"Frank! Frank Bratton!"

At the sound of his name being called from the upper gallery of the saloon, Bratton halted, glancing toward the speaker.

"It's me. Monty Killeen."

Killeen. A man from out of the past. Once they had run together, pulling a few holdups, drifting around while their following grew into a small gang, and then, because of the law and certain other reasons, Bratton had lost contact with him.

"Come on up here! There are some folks who'll be plenty glad to see you!" Killeen continued, and then called to the bartender, "Pete, this fellow's a special friend of mine. Send that breakfast he ordered up to my room. Put it on my tab."

Reluctant to renew the relationship, Bratton nevertheless mounted the steps and joined Killeen, pausing at the top of the flight to shake his hand and clap him soundly on the shoulder. Maybe it would be a bit of good luck; he'd be in Turkey Springs but a short while to hide out, and Monty Killeen's quarters would be far safer than being down in the saloon.

"Been a long time—three years, I figure—since I saw you," Monty said, taking Frank by the arm and shepherding him down a hallway. "Never did get the chance to thank you for going to jail for us when we got caught robbing that bank. We were all mighty grateful."

Bratton downed the drink he was carrying and shrugged. "Long time ago," he said, dismissing the subject.

Monty had changed little over the years. His intelligence still showed through, and he dressed as flashy as ever. Handsome in a dark, smooth way with chestnut-colored hair, blue eyes, clipped mustache, and a wide smile, Monty had the faculty for making friends easily and invariably had his way with any woman to whom he took a fancy.

"Wondered every now and then what had become of you—"

"I keep moving, mostly," Bratton replied, "playing the houses and the casinos."

"You always were mighty good with a deck of cards," Monty said. "Have you done all right?"

"Not complaining," Frank replied.

"Well, I'm real pleased to run into you," Killeen said, halting at the last door along the corridor. "I've got a deal on the fire that'll be right to your liking."

Bratton hesitated. "Don't figure to be here long, Monty," he began, but Killeen waved him into silence.

"Now don't say no until you heard what I've got lined up. Meantime, I want you to meet the rest of the bunch."

Bratton started to say more but fell silent as Killeen flung the door wide and pushed him into the sitting room, made larger by a connecting hallway into the bedroom.

"See here what I found, folks!" Monty shouted. "Just take a look at what I spotted downstairs drinking all by his lonesome—our old friend Frank Bratton!"

Four men turned toward Bratton. He recognized familiar faces through the smoke haze that hung in the room. Beyond the men were two women. Bratton stiffened slightly as the taller of the two came around and faced him. His jaw hardened, and he swore softly.

Jenny McCall. She was the last person, other than Harry Locke, that he wanted to see.

CHAPTER 5

MONTY KILLEEN SMILED SLYLY AS HE NOTICED THE change in Bratton's expression. "You know Jenny—and you know the boys. The other lady, however, is a sort of newcomer to the outfit. Name's Becky."

Frank nodded slightly to the girl and moved deeper into the room, stuffy from the heat and the smell of liquor and stale tobacco smoke. Shifting his eyes to the men, he bucked his head at Monty's brother Sid—a younger edition of the gang leader. Sid had changed little in three years. He still had that cocky, impatient way about him.

27

"Good to see you," he said coolly, shaking Frank's hand.

Bratton shrugged. He and Sid had never seen eye to eye on anything. Moving on, Frank reached out to the next man in line.

"Howdy, Kurt."

Kurt Zeller, sharp-faced, wearing a gray suit and a stained white shirt with a red necktie, grinned as he took Bratton's hand into his own.

"I'm mighty glad to see you, Frank!" he said, exposing uneven, yellowed teeth. "Could've used you and that iron of yours a couple of times."

When Kurt released his grip on Bratton's fingers, Augie Vinson took a step forward. He was young, dark-featured, and had the easy, careless ways of a cowhand.

"Reckon Kurt's said it all excepting maybe to thank you for doing what you done for us after that bank holdup," Augie said.

The robbery had cost him two years of his life, Bratton thought, but there was no point in bringing up that fact. Nothing could be done about it now, and the bitterness he had once felt had long since faded.

"Forget it," he murmured.

He supposed it should feel good to be among old friends again, even though they no longer had similar ideas or followed the same trails. But somehow it didn't feel good, he realized, as he shook hands with the fourth man, Dollar Smith. Dollar, who was somewhat backward and slow of mind, still wore the silver coin around his neck that had given him the nickname of which he was so proud.

"Was a pleasure seeing you boys before I ride on," Bratton said then, with no particular cordiality. "I—"

"Ride on!" Monty Killeen echoed. "Hell, partner, you

28

can't do that!"

But Frank Bratton only half heard Killeen's words. Unable to ignore Jenny McCall any further, his attention was now on her. Although a bit older, she was still an attractive woman. Her eyes were as clear as always—the brightest blue he had ever seen. Her hair was just as dark, an almost raven black, while her nose had the same saucy tip, just as he had often remembered. The plain gray dress she now wore did not conceal the curves of her figure. Despite her youthful appearance, there was an overall change in her, he had to admit; the happiness was gone, and sadness showed in the droop of her lips.

"Hello, Frank," she greeted in her quiet way.

"It's good to see you, Jenny," he said, unable to think of other words to say.

Once they had been close. So close that marriage had been the next step in their lives. Then Monty Killeen entered the scene and turned on his charm. They had grown apart after that, and when it became apparent that Jenny had eyes only for Monty, Frank waited for the right opportunity to quit the gang, to move on. The unsuccessful bank robbery had brought the split sooner than he'd expected. . . .

"Nice to see you again," Jenny responded. "This is Becky."

Becky was young, no more than sixteen or seventeen, very pretty and well shaped. She had large brown eyes and light hair and was dressed in a red dress that exposed much of her bosom as well as her lace-stockinged legs. Probably Sid Killeen's woman, Frank guessed.

"Pleased to meet you," Bratton said, inclining his head slightly.

29

"Same here," Becky responded, smiling. "You an old friend of Monty's?"

"Yeah, we go back a ways," Killeen said before Bratton could speak. "All of us do. Once we had us a real outfit going, till bad luck hit us one day and Frank wound up in the pen."

"Heard you'd got out and had gone straight," Sid Killeen said. "Kind of hard to believe an old hell-raiser like you turning sweet as honey."

Monty laughed. "Expect you'll find that this honey's got a bite to it," he said, and paused as a knock on the door sounded. Wheeling, he opened the scarred panel to admit one of the saloon swampers bearing a tray with the breakfast Bratton had ordered.

"Put it on the table there, Louie," Killeen directed, pointing.

The swamper hastened to comply, grinning broadly as Monty flipped a coin to him, and then beat a hurried retreat.

"Sit down and do your eating," Monty said, nodding to Bratton. "I'll do my talking while you're at it.... Rest of you go on downstairs or do something, but leave us alone."

Vinson and Kurt Zeller, always eager to please Monty, started for the door at once. The two women moved off into the adjoining room. Sid Killeen, however, did not stir.

"I want to know something before I get out of here," he said, facing his brother. "You figuring on cutting him in on the deal?"

Monty pulled up a chair for Bratton and then drew another close for his own use. Straddling it, he finally acknowledged his brother's pointed question with a cold look.

30

"You taking over this outfit, kid?"

Dollar Smith, arms folded across his thick chest, head thrust forward belligerently, nodded vigorously. "I'm wanting to know about that, too!"

Monty favored the dim-witted man patronizingly. "About what, dummy?"

Dollar shifted nervously. "About what Sid's asking, and don't call me that, Monty. You know I don't like it."

"Splitting what we'll get four ways will be satisfactory," Sid declared. "I ain't for making it five."

"Your share of the cash will be more money than you've ever seen in your life, no matter how it's cut," Monty said, and motioned to Becky, who was listening in the doorway to the adjoining room. "Bring the bottle over here. And a glass."

Becky crossed to a washstand on the opposite side of the room, took up a half-full bottle of whiskey and a glass, and handed them to Killeen. Frank, hungry, had begun to eat, enjoying the steak and fried potatoes, the still warm buttered and honeyed biscuits, and the coffee.

"You're mighty handy to have around," he heard Monty say as he wrapped an arm around the girl's waist. "Just don't know how I ever got along without you."

Frank slid a covert glance at the inner doorway. Jenny would be just inside. No doubt she would have heard what Killeen had said, but she was apparently not going to make any issue of it. Was she forced to play second fiddle to Becky or did the young blonde belong to Sid or one of the other men, as he thought? It could be that Monty was just taking his usual liberties.

"Now you get yourself out of here," Killeen said, slapping the girl affectionately on the buttocks. "Bratton and me've got some important talking to do.... Goes for

31

you men, too," he added to his brother and Dollar Smith.

"I ain't going nowhere till I know what you're up to," the younger Killeen declared flatly as Becky joined Jenny in the next room. "If you're thinking to—"

Monty Killeen rose suddenly, seizing Sid by the arm and shoving him roughly toward the hall doorway, left open by Zeller and Vinson.

"When you're top hand of this outfit, you can talk like that!" he snarled, eyes bright with anger. "You, too, Dollar. Both of you—get the hell out of here and if you can't find anything to do, go take a bath. Both smell like you need one."

Dollar, mumbling unintelligibly, picked up a hat hung on a chair back, jammed it on his balding head, and walked stiffly by Monty to join Sid Killeen in the corridor.

"Now maybe you and me can get down to business without any more butting in," Monty said, resuming his place.

Harry Locke glared at the two Rangers. "Got you birds to thank for losing my prisoner—" he began.

"Now, don't you go blaming us, Marshal!" Tom Vogel broke in sharply. "Was you that didn't have the irons on him like you should've!"

They had patrolled back and forth for hours along the border, spoken with the Mexican soldiers stationed along the line, and turned up no signs of Frank Bratton.

Now, back in the settlement and gathered in front of the saloon, they were heatedly blaming each other for Bratton's escape.

"Weren't necessary," Locke snapped. "Had his gun."

"Recollect you saying you knew him—like, maybe he

32

was a friend," Billy Jay Coleman said slyly. "Well, he sure wasn't one I'd want."

"Me neither," Vogel added.

Locke swore impatiently. "Never said he was a friend—only that I knew him. And he'd still be my prisoner if you two hadn't horned in, all lathered up wanting to make things look good for yourselves! Well, you won't be getting no glory out of this! I'll see that your captain hears all about what you done."

Coleman drew up in alarm. "Now, just a minute here, Marshal. There ain't no need—"

"Forget it," Vogel cut in. "He won't be telling the captain anything he won't already know. I aim to make a full report first off and set things straight myself."

Harry Locke hawked and spat into the dust. "I'll just bet you will," he said, and turned away.

He was simply wasting time jawing with those Rangers. Better he put the minutes into trying to learn which direction Frank Bratton had taken when he'd left town. Spurring his horse lightly, the lawman circled around to the stable. The hostler met him as he entered the runway.

"Couldn't you catch him, Marshal?"

"Wasn't no sign of him anywhere," Locke replied. "I need to ask you some questions."

"Sure thing. What happened to them damn Rangers? That one that fired a shot at your prisoner scared hell out of my horses."

"They've gone on, Coaley. You happen to know which way my prisoner—name's Bratton—went when he rode out?"

"Towards the border—"

"Know that. I mean later. He had to've doubled back this way and then rode on out of town. Figured maybe

33

you or somebody else might've seen him going by."

"No, I sure didn't, Marshal. It's my guess he lined out for El Paso. Plenty of places to hide there."

"That's probably what Bratton wants me to think," Locke decided after a few moments' consideration. Then, "You see anybody sort of ambling around in the last couple of hours? I ain't talking about Bratton. I'm talking about townspeople or customers of Thorne's or the saloon. Lots of folks like to stroll around in the evening, get themselves some fresh air."

"Can't say as I did, but I stick pretty close to the barn most of the time. Lots of these jaspers try to skin me out of money for taking care of their animals by just slipping in and saddling up and riding off without so much as a 'go to hell' or an 'adios.'"

"Plenty of crooks around, all right—"

"For a fact. Now, I was just thinking, you might sashay over to the back of the saloon. I've seen folks setting out there on the back landing, spooning and such, a few times. There just might've been somebody out there when that killer rode off—if'n he come this way."

Harry Locke nodded. "That's just what I'll do, Coaley. Sure obliged to you," he said and, swinging his sorrel around again, struck for the rear of the saloon.

Maybe he'd have some luck there. A couple, or perhaps a man stepping outside for a few moments to get the smoke out of his lungs, might recall seeing a lone rider angling north across the flats. If not, the lawman thought, sighing heavily, he'd have to start from scratch, and by the time he'd gotten through talking to everyone who might have seen Frank Bratton, the outlaw could be a hundred miles away.

CHAPTER 6

FOR A LONG MINUTE MONTY KILLEEN WATCHED Bratton at work eating his breakfast, and then, as Frank paused to take a swallow of coffee, he drew a sack of tobacco and a fold of brown papers from his shirt pocket and began to roll a cigarette.

"You on the run?" he asked, considering Bratton with a side glance.

"Maybe," Bratton said with a shrug, setting his cup back on the tray.

Monty Killeen had always possessed the faculty for sizing up a man and determining what the score was with him.

"Maybe—hell!" Killeen said with a laugh. "I can see it sticking out all over you! Who's trailing you and what for?"

Frank settled back, accepted the makings from Monty, and made a smoke for himself. He could hear one of the women moving around in the adjoining room, and from the lower floor of the Valley Rose came the mutter of voices punctuated now and then by laughter. Returning the tobacco and papers, he leaned forward as Monty held a lighted match for him. Bratton sucked the slim brown cylinder into life.

"Harry Locke—a deputy U.S. Marshal. I killed a tinhorn down near the border."

"Charlie Thorne's place?"

Frank nodded. "Tinhorn's name was Jace Madden. Could be you know him."

"Nope, never heard of him. Happens I do know that old lawdog, however. How come he's after you for putting under a cardsharp?"

35

"I couldn't prove he was cheating and having been in the pen didn't help me much."

"No, I reckon it wouldn't. How'd you give Locke the slip?"

"A couple of Texas Rangers tried to take over," Bratton said, and related the incident that made it possible for him to escape. "I'm headed for a town in the northeast corner of Texas...my folks' home—"

"Yeh, Lipscomb. I remember you talking about it—"

"Figure to lay low there for a spell, then when things've quieted down, ride back to Charlie's Place and make Thorne own up to lying about what happened. Only way I can clear my name."

"Should've made the marshal do that while you were there. His job—"

Bratton brushed away the sweat collected on his forehead. The room was hot, and stuffy. "Said he would. Big rub was that I had to lay it out in jail while he did. Could've meant weeks, maybe longer, and I don't want any more of that."

"Can't blame you there," Monty said. "That all you've been doing for the past year—playing cards?"

Frank shrugged. There was a slight movement in the doorway to the connecting room, and he caught a glimpse of Jenny McCall's shoulder. Evidently, she had been listening. "Easy way to make a living," he responded.

"Well, I've got a better way," Killeen declared. "One that'll really pay off—"

"Expect Harry Locke's close on my trail now," Bratton interrupted. "I'm not about to let him catch up."

"This'll only take a day, maybe even less."

Bratton frowned. The cigarette he'd made had died and now hung limply from a corner of his mouth. "No, reckon I'll keep going, Monty. Obliged to you just the same."

"What the hell are you so jumpy about? If you're still as good with your gun as you used to be, you don't need to let Locke or any other lawman run you off from a good deal. What's one tin star less in the country, anyway?"

Jenny was no longer visible in the doorway. Likely she realized she was being seen and had drawn back out of sight. The racket coming from below had increased in volume, and somewhere nearby in the settlement, children were playing, their shrill voices floating in through the open windows as they shouted and laughed.

"Backed off using my gun since I got out of the pen—"

Killeen tossed his cigarette stub aside and started a fresh one. "Thought you said you killed a gambler down along the border?"

"Did. Clubbed him. Was no gunplay."

"Well," Monty said, lighting up again, "I expect you'll change your mind when I tell you what I've got schemed up. Your share'd be ten thousand dollars, more or less."

"A holdup?"

"Yeh—the express office of a stagecoach outfit over in Flatrock. Town about a half-day's ride east of here."

"I know where it is."

"I got word, straight, that the stage'll be bringing in fifty thousand dollars, maybe more, in cash tomorrow afternoon. It's for some big mining outfit. Agent at the station will put it in the safe and hold it overnight.

"I don't look for any kind of a ruckus. Fact is, there'll only be the station agent and a couple of helpers. I expect a couple of guards, too. I figure to slip in after

37

dark, take care of the agent and whoever else's there, and blow the door off the safe. Ought to get it all done in an hour or less."

"Sounds like you've got it all figured out real good," Bratton said, "but it's not for me. I've kept my nose clean ever since I got out of the pen and—"

"Except for killing that gambler . . ."

Frank nodded. "And I aim to clear myself of that. Anyway, the station agent over at Flatrock's a good friend of mine from way back. Name's Gillberg. Done me a couple of favors once. I'm not about to give him trouble."

"Not even for ten thousand dollars?"

"Nope. Could use that kind of money for sure—but it's not that big to me."

Killeen now swiped at the sweat on his face, using his handkerchief while he studied Bratton with puzzled eyes. After a bit he shrugged.

"Hell, you wouldn't have to run up against this Gillberg. Sid could take care of him. Your job would to handle the four or five guards the stage line's leaving there."

Frank laughed. It was the Monty of old. "Thought you said there'd be only a couple of guards."

Killeen's shoulders stirred indifferently. "Expect there'll only be a couple in the office. The stage outfit'll have a few more outside two or three at the most. Then besides the station agent—Gillberg or whatever his name is—there's a couple of hostlers. Didn't figure it'd make any difference to you how many there were around—leastwise, it wouldn't to the Frank Bratton that I rode with a while back."

Bratton took up the bottle of whiskey, poured himself a drink. He was silently cursing his luck for having run into Monty Killeen—and Jenny McCall.

"Don't you go fretting over what Sid and the dummy had to say about the split. They'll do what they're told and take what I give them, and if they don't like it—them or any of the others—they know damn well what they can do.

"But we won't have any problem with them once they've thought about it. They're not too dumb to realize we need a gun hand like you. They'll go for the idea."

Frank stared at the dust-clouded window, which looked out over an adjoining building. Ten thousand dollars was a lot of money. But earning it would put him right back where he was a few years before—always looking over his shoulder for some lawman. He had grown accustomed to not worrying about that since serving the last stretch in the pen, and it had been a good, comfortable way of life. He shook his head.

"Obliged to you, Monty, for the offer, but—"

"Do some tall thinking about it, partner. It's your chance to put yourself in high clover. You could take your split, ride on to Lipscomb, and take it easy there in style for as long as you wanted. Doubt if you're exactly flush right now."

"Got three, maybe four hundred, in my pocket—"

"That won't last long. I haven't met a gambler yet who wasn't flat busted or nearly so. With the kind of money you'd be getting you could, why, hell, you could set up your own game somewhere. . . . How do you get to this place you're headed for—Lipscomb?"

"From here I figure to keep going north till I come to Cabezone, a town on the west side of Apache Mountain. Then I'll cut across to the other side, to Buckeye, another town. If Locke's on my trail and I'm mighty damn sure he is—he'll think I kept going north from Cabezone and stayed on that side of the mountain. Aim to make it look like that, anyway."

"That'll fix it so's you can cut across the Staked Plain country for Texas and head on north."

Bratton nodded. "I'm hoping that's how it'll work out, but Harry Locke's a smart one. Maybe it'll fool him and maybe it won't. The big thing is, I've got to stay ahead of him."

"When are you planning to move on—if you're not throwing in with me?"

"Noon at the latest. Had to give my horse a little rest. Once I get to Cabezone and head up the mountain, I'll be able to take it a little easier."

"You will if the marshal swallows your trick—"

Frank shrugged. "Always was a good hand at covering my tracks."

"Maybe you haven't thought of it, but Locke could have already caught up with you and be here in Turkey Springs right now."

"Chance he is, of course, but I doubt it. I got a pretty fair start on him last night."

Monty filled his glass from the bottle, tossed off the fiery liquor in a single motion, and slumped in his chair.

"Still say you're making a big mistake," he said resignedly, "but I reckon if you're set on riding out at noon, that's your privilege. What say we go downstairs and play a few hands of cards with the boys while you're waiting?"

"Suits me," Bratton replied, also pushing back his chair and getting to his feet. "Always a pleasure to welcome fresh money."

"You haven't won it yet," Killeen said good-naturedly as they moved for the door.

CHAPTER 7

"YOU GETTING YOUR EAR FULL, HONEY?"

At Becky's caustic question Jenny turned away from the doorway. In reality she had not been listening particularly to what was being said between Frank Bratton and Killeen but was more interested in just looking at Frank.

"What're they talking about?" Becky continued, throwing herself across the bed as Jenny sat down on the rocking chair and began to move back and forth idly.

"I wasn't paying much mind, but I think Monty's trying to get Frank to throw in with us again."

"Again?"

"He was a good friend of Monty's—of all of us once."

Becky considered Jenny closely. "More than just a friend where you're concerned, I suspect."

Jenny shrugged. "Yes, there was a time—"

"Well, he sure ain't much for looks—I can say that about him. Nothing like Monty."

Anger surged through Jenny McCall She ought to get up and slap the little hussy silly for saying that! Maybe Frank wasn't as handsome as Monty Killeen, but he was ten times the man!

That had been her mistake, Jenny thought. Falling for Monty's surface charms. Once she had been Frank Bratton's woman, and then Monty had taken it upon himself to center his attentions on her and she had foolishly responded. Eventually she and Frank had split, and not long after that, Monty had led them all in a bank robbery attempt. Something had gone wrong, and Frank had been caught and sent to the pen.

41

A south Missouri girl, Jenny had met Frank in St. Louis where she was working in a saloon. It wasn't what she wanted, but both her parents had died when the family home burned down, leaving her with little more than the clothes on her back and enough cash to make her way to the big city on the Mississippi where she expected to find a job.

She met Frank Bratton about a week after she arrived. He was with Monty Killeen and three other men, and they took to each other right off. A short time after that, when Frank and the rest decided to move on, he asked her to come with them. She had readily agreed. It didn't matter to her that they were outlaws, that they lived by holding up stagecoaches, robbing stores and a bank; what did matter was that she was with Frank Bratton.

Nor did it trouble her Baptist upbringing that marriage was never in the picture. They simply lived as man and wife, enjoying the other's company and giving no consideration to the future. Her state of euphoria existed for almost a year, and then Monty had changed. He became more attentive, always exhibiting the genteel ways he'd been accustomed to before breaking Connecticut family ties and going west to live the kind of carefree life that beckoned.

Monty had never done anything behind Bratton's back; he had too much respect for Frank's fast gun and hard-as-iron ways. But in the end he had filled her with a sort of dissatisfaction, and she had drawn away from Frank, and almost before she realized what was happening, he was gone from her life.

Now he was back—at least partially so. She had no way of knowing if he would rejoin Monty and the others, but she hoped so. Then, perhaps, they could pick up where she had so foolishly allowed them to break off.

Monty had lost interest in her in little more than a year. She should have seen it coming. He'd never been the man Frank was, lacking the quiet, cool courtesy that she had appreciated so much. While Monty had not been really hard on her, he'd slapped her around pretty much a few times when he was drunk. When he had met Becky in a Fort Worth saloon not too many months ago, she had actually welcomed the girl taking over as his woman; it freed her from having to put up with any more of his demands.

Of course, she had become fair game then for Sid Killeen and all the rest of the men in the gang, and while she was able to fend them off, it became necessary, and practical, to give in to Sid on occasion, just to protect herself from the others. As Monty's brother was considered second in command, and thus the inheritor of Monty's leftovers—which naturally included his women.

Jenny managed the best she could. A survivor, she met her problems a day at a time and was looking forward to a chance to leave the gang—an opportunity she believed would come when they visited one of the large cities, preferably Denver. She had relatives there, distant ones admittedly, but their family ties were strong, and she knew she would get help if she asked.

But now, seeing Frank Bratton, Jenny was beginning to doubt her ability to put up with Monty and his followers much longer. Seeing him had reawakened all her earlier feelings for him, and while she could detect no similar emotion for her in his manner, she had hope.

And hoping would make it all the more difficult to continue the life she was leading. It wasn't too bad for her when Monty halted in a town and they put up in a

43

hotel or an inn. He usually occupied one room with Becky while Sid, who stayed drunk most of the time, occupied another with her. A third was shared by Vinson, Dollar Smith, and Kurt Zeller. It was when they had to camp along a trail somewhere that it was bad.

Sid was only a pale shadow of his brother in every way and, far from looking after her as he should, she generally ended up with a pistol in her hands, warding off simpleminded Dollar Smith or one of the others while Sid lay nearby in a drunken stupor.

Jenny returned to the present and glanced at Becky. The girl had dozed off. Rising, Jenny moved to the doorway. Frank and Monty Killeen were still talking, their voices low and barely audible.

"Maybe you haven't thought of it, but Locke could have already caught up with you and is here in Turkey Springs right now."

Monty's words struck a note of fear in Jenny. Frank was in trouble of some kind—serious trouble if a U.S. Marshal was on his trail.

Bratton made a reply, most of it lost because of his low voice, but Jenny did distinguish enough words to know that he figured he was well ahead of the lawman.

Monty was clearly dissatisfied with the meeting. Frank had refused to join with him in the proposed stagecoach way-station robbery. Jenny, however, was both relieved and disappointed at Bratton's decision. Hope for a reconciliation had glimmered within her, but on the other hand, she knew Monty well enough to recognize the deep hatred he had for Frank. And she realized that if something went wrong at the Flatrock holdup, he would manage somehow to saddle Bratton with the blame so that he and the others could go free.

"Still say you're making a big mistake, but I reckon if

44

you're set on riding out at noon, that's your privilege. ."

Killeen said more, and Frank replied, but Jenny's mind was closed to them. Frank would be leaving at noon, Monty had indicated—and that had sent her already sagging spirits plummeting further. Numbly she heard the scrape of chair legs on the floor as the men rose, the sound of their boot heels on the bare floor as they crossed to the door, opened it, stepped out into the hallway, and pulled the panel shut. Only then did her mind begin to function again.

Where was Frank Bratton headed? Just what kind of trouble was he in? Would he welcome her as a trail partner should she choose this moment to break away from Monty and his bunch? Or would he turn his back on her as she had so foolishly done to him three years ago?

Sighing dejectedly and with no answers to any of her self-imposed questions, Jenny returned to the rocking chair in the adjoining room and sat down. At low ebb, she struggled to disentangle the bitter thoughts crowding her mind and to decide what she should do.

Jenny was still there an hour later when Sid Killeen, well liquored up as usual, entered the room and demanded that she come with him.

CHAPTER 8

FRANK BRATTON LEFT THE VALLEY ROSE A FEW minutes past noon and walked the short distance to the livery barn where he had stabled his horse. He had taken but little interest in the poker game organized by Monty Killeen, his mind on Deputy Marshal Harry Locke. And Jenny McCall.

Locke would be somewhere nearby if he had gotten on the trail within a few hours. That the marshal had searched around until he learned what he needed to know—which direction his escaping prisoner had taken—was a certainty, for Harry Locke was that kind of a dedicated lawman. The only question remaining was how far behind Locke could be, a half day or a half hour, and Bratton realized he would know the answer to that only when he caught sight of the marshal. That was the worst thing about it—the not knowing.

Perhaps he shouldn't have laid over in Turkey Springs, even for a short time. Maybe he should have just kept going, pushing his horse until the animal could go no farther. But such could have put him on foot, and a man caught without a horse in the endless, open country of New Mexico territory was as good as dead. No, it was better that he trust his gambler instincts and risk a few hours for the sake of the bay. Then he would ride on. So far it looked as if his decision had paid off. He let his mind wander in a different direction.

Jenny McCall . . . He had watched for her during the time he was playing cards expecting, or possibly hoping, that she would put in an appearance, but she had not. Maybe she didn't want to see him and had no thought of getting things started between them again, although it was clear she and Monty Killeen were no longer paired off.

Monty had evidently picked himself up a new girl and had cut Jenny out. But Jenny was still with the bunch, which could only mean that she had taken up with one of the other men. Jenny didn't look to be very happy, probably because Becky had taken her place with Monty—or it could be that his return had awakened old and unwanted memories. Whatever the cause, Jenny had

46

made no effort to seek him out. He reckoned that her silence told him how she felt.

But it had been good to see her, and the encounter, brief as it was, had brought alive a host of good recollections that he thought he'd laid to rest a long time ago. Just looking at her stirred him deeply, as it always had. Bratton swore softly. He wished now he hadn't seen Jenny McCall; for his part, he would have been better off.

Reaching the livery barn, Frank paused and threw his glance to the south. Locke would be coming up that road if he hadn't already arrived, and was somewhere in the settlement—which didn't seem likely. The road was clear with no sign of any travelers; but that, too, was not wholly reassuring. If the marshal were playing it cagey, he would avoid riding in the open and would stick to the brushy trail along the river where he wouldn't be easily seen.

"Your horse is ready, mister," a voice called from the stable runway. "Took good care of him—just like you was wanting me to."

With a final look toward the far end of town, Bratton moved into the stable. The bay was waiting for him in the first stall, fed, watered, and shining after a brisk rubdown.

"He ain't hardly had enough rest," the hostler said. "Could tell from feeling his legs. Expect you ought to wait for dark before your ride out—if you can."

"That's what I'd do if I had the time," Frank replied, reaching into his pocket. "What do I owe you?"

"I reckon a dollar'll be enough."

Bratton handed over the specified coin and swung up into the saddle. Settling himself, he looked down at the overall-clad stableman.

47

"There been anybody ride in since I got here? I'm looking for somebody from the south. Or maybe the west," Bratton added. Harry Locke might circle wide to make it look as if he weren't coming up from the border.

"Nope, sure ain't. One of the hands that works on a ranch right close come in looking for the doc. Got hisself throwed. Hurt some. Other'n him—"

"Much obliged," Frank broke in, wheeling the bay around. Digging into his pocket again, he produced another silver dollar and tossed it to the hostler. "That's to pay for keeping your mouth shut if a man shows up and asks about me."

The hostler's face was split with a wide grin. "Sure, sure—I ain't seen you or nobody else! What'll this fellow look like?"

"He'll be a U.S. Marshal," Frank said, and as the smile faded from the stableman's face and was replaced by a troubled frown, he continued, "Don't fret about that part of it. All you've got to say is no."

The hostler lowered his head, eyes on the silver coins in his gnarled hand. "Well, all right. I ain't much for lying, but I reckon I can just sort of keep my lip buttoned if he asks. Which way you headed?"

Frank withheld a smile. It was what he wanted the hostler to ask. "North. To Cabezone," he said, and, nodding to the man, rode the bay gelding out of the stable and turned onto the road. Now, regardless of how the stableman reacted when Harry Locke questioned him, as he surely would, the lawman would be put on the right trail.

Clouds had gathered along the eastern horizon and were climbing slowly into the sky's blue arch. The smell of rain was in the air, and it occurred to Bratton that most likely he'd get wet long before he reached

Cabezone, where he planned to throw Harry Locke off his trail by sending him farther north.

Chances were good that his scheme would work, unless the rain came and wiped out the tracks he intended to leave once he arrived at the settlement. Best he double his chances at success by dropping a few words around for the lawman's benefit, he decided. Just a few, however; he couldn't afford to make Locke suspicious. Then it would be east across the mountain to Buckeye, and from there, after a bit of rest, on to the Staked Plain country, and then Lipscomb.

The thought of Lipscomb filled Frank with a rush of memories. Lipscomb lay along Wolf Creek, high in the northeast corner of the panhandle, only a frog's jump, as his pa used to say, from Indian territory. His folks came from a breed filled with the pioneering spirit, and they had looked for a new world in which freedom from all restraints of any kind was paramount. Selling off their holdings in Iowa, the Brattons had moved west while Frank was still a youngster.

They had settled along Wolf Creek where Adam Bratton, with the aid of his wife, Zora, and Frank's older brother began to farm wheat and sorghum cane, which the land seemed most adapted to. In time, hogs and a few head of cattle were brought in, and the scope of the Bratton homestead broadened.

Frank had enjoyed growing up there, doing his share of the back-breaking work without complaint, but as more people settled in the area and a town began to form, he contracted the same fever of restlessness that had overcome his parents. One day, just after his eighteenth birthday, Frank announced his decision to ride on.

Both his mother and brother endeavored to dissuade

him. But his father, seeing himself in his young son and understanding the urge that gripped him, gave Frank his blessing, along with a horse and a bit of cash—ten dollars that he'd been saving for an emergency.

Frank had never returned to the farm, although he had fully intended to. Something always turned up, it seemed, forcing a change of plans and delaying the visit. He didn't know for certain if his parents were still alive—they would be well on in years by now and the brutal, endless labor of making the land pay had a way of shortening the lives of those who undertook it.

A light sprinkle of rain began to fall when Frank was a mile away from Cabezone, the settlement at the southwest corner of sprawling, lush Apache Mountain.

Coming into the town, he sought out the general store and, in need of ammunition for his six-gun, entered and made the purchase. He spent a few minutes with the storekeeper, asking about the road north and the towns he would encounter en route to Colorado. The merchant was cooperative as well as talkative, and when Bratton returned to his horse, he knew the man could give Locke not only a good description of him but also a full knowledge of where he intended to go and the road he was taking to get there.

But there was no guarantee that Harry Locke would accept the storekeeper's information, even if the marshal halted there to ask about the passage of a stranger. Yet it seemed logical the lawman would. If Locke reached Cabezone, it would mean he had talked to the hostler in Turkey Springs and had then taken the road north. And, if he thus had questioned the hostler, there was no reason to doubt he would talk to the Cabezone storekeeper as well. He would conclude he was on the right trail and continue north.

50

And north Frank Bratton went. Mounting the weary bay, and with a light drizzle of rain falling, he followed the road out of the settlement for five miles or so, to a point where a creek made a gravelly crossing. There he cut hard right and started up over the mountain for Buckeye, the town that lay on the opposite side.

He didn't have far to ride, although climbing the mountain, fairly steep in this area, would be difficult for the gelding, already weary from the ride up from Turkey Springs. He'd pull off somewhere on the slope and let the bay rest. The fact of the matter was that he could use a bit of a break himself. It seemed to him like he'd been in the saddle for days, but he reckoned that would end now. Harry Locke would soon be off his trail, and he could stop for a while in Buckeye and then be on his way to Lipscomb.

It would be good to see the family again. He'd stay with them for a time, long enough to let things cool down, and then return to Charlie's Place. With Locke somewhere in Colorado searching for him and not yet ready to start backtracking to see where he'd lost his escaped prisoner's trail, he would have time to get Charlie Thorne cornered and force him to admit to the Rangers that Jace Madden's death had been accidental and that Bratton had struck him in self-defense.

Then he'd be in the clear once more and could resume the way of life he preferred—drifting around the country making his living at the poker tables.

CHAPTER 9

SEVERAL TIMES DURING THE RIDE BETWEEN TURKEY Springs and Cabezone, Frank Bratton had paused to

51

study his back trail. Not once had he caught sight of a rider, and now, as he rode up the narrow trail leading across Apache Mountain to the town of Buckeye, his feelings of security insofar as Harry Locke was concerned mounted.

Evidently the marshal had found it hard to get a line on him, which was exactly the way Frank had wanted it to be. He'd taken care to ride unseen out of Charlie's Place, and he reckoned he had succeeded except, perhaps, for the couple who were on the back landing of the saloon. But they were so engrossed in each other that he was almost dead certain now that they had not noticed him.

Likely Locke had spent the rest of the night and well into the next day asking questions as he sought to solve the puzzle of where his escaping prisoner had gone. He may have convinced himself that his man had gone to El Paso where there were hundreds of hiding places. If so, the lawman would waste several days there before he decided he was on the wrong trail. All of that would work in his favor, Bratton knew, and would give him more than enough time to reach Lipscomb.

He supposed, instead of taking it upon himself to clear his name, that he could have put the whole affair in the hands of Harry Locke, but he couldn't bear the thought of sitting it out in a cell in El Paso, Turkey Springs, or any other town they might send him to for safekeeping. Even one day behind bars would be too much.

No, he had done the right thing, he decided. He was now free to work at clearing his name himself, and this he would do just as soon as he felt it was safe to start and he would be able to do it without the relentless, hunched figure of Harry Locke dogging his tracks. By the time the lawman got through sorting out leads in Colorado, he would be back at the border, bringing Charlie Thorne to task before the Rangers.

The rain continued, and pulling his poncho from the roll tied to the back of his saddle, Frank drew it on. Frank felt pleasant being slightly wet, not cold but comfortably cool, and he knew he would just as soon continue on through the night until he reached Buckeye. But the bay was laboring under the climb up the mountain, and he reckoned it was best to halt, make camp, and let the big gelding rest for a few hours. Without the immediate threat of Deputy Marshal Harry Locke, he did not have to hurry.

Near the crest of the slope, the smell of smoke reached Bratton. Could be a camp of some kind, belonging either to Indians or pilgrims who had pulled up to await daylight. But caution was an inbred trait in Bratton's character, and moving carefully and quietly, he worked his way through the trees and brush until he located the fire, a dull red glow in the wet darkness.

He would just as soon encounter no one, in the event that any traveler or travelers headed on west met Harry Locke after they descended the mountain and were asked if they had seen a lone rider somewhere along the way. The same held true if it were a party of Apache or Comanche Indians. Since they were now on more or less friendly terms with the white people, they would cooperate with the law if approached.

But the fire had not been started by Indians or pilgrims. Riding quietly and halting at a safe distance, Bratton had a long look at the camp. Three grizzled and hard-looking men were hunched under a square of canvas strung between four trees. A fitful fire struggled to maintain itself inside the edge of the bellying tarp just

53

out of reach of the drizzle. A few strides beyond the flickering, circle of light, three horses, hip-shot and with heads hung low, were weathering the rain in the open.

Outlaws. Cat-eyed curly wolves, Bratton concluded, sizing up the men and their gear. He'd run across their kind many times in the past. They hung around the trails, preying on pilgrims passing by. It seemed to Frank that this bunch would have slim pickings on such a seldom-used trail as this one crossing Apache Mountain, but it could be that they were on the move and, getting caught by the rain, had holed up for the night.

Continuing on his way unnoticed, Frank rode for another hour and then a short distance down the opposite side of the mountain, drew off into the brush, and made camp. The rains had stopped, but everything was wet, and he could do little more than to huddle under the overhang of a low bluff while nearby, the bay caught up on rest.

Well before first light, Bratton was again in the saddle and moving off the slope. He was anxious now to reach Buckeye. Wet and cold from the early-morning chill, he was anxious to treat himself to a couple of stiff drinks, get into some dry clothing, and have a good, hot meal—all in that order.

He would have to lay over there, too, for a short time, just as he had done in Turkey Springs, and let the bay rest, but that would pose no problem. He was sure Harry Locke was out of the picture now, and the horse should have at least a day's respite before heading out across the Staked Plain country and on north to Lipscomb.

Around midmorning he rode into Buckeye, a scattering of ten or twelve stores, saloons, and other necessary structures. The rain had ceased, although the sky was still threatening, and with that in mind he exchanged the poncho for the wool jacket rolled in his blanket.

There were few people in evidence as he walked the bay slowly down the center of the street in search of a livery stable. He was taking no particular precautions now, for, if all had gone as Frank was certain it would, the lawman would be following the road that skirted the west side of Apache Mountain—if he had managed to catch up that much—on his way north to Colorado.

Frank spotted the sign he was looking for above the open doorway of a sprawling, red-painted building a short distance on down the wide street. COOPER'S LIVERY STABLE, it read. There was a saloon on beyond it, he noted, not the largest and most ornate in the town but one that should satisfy his needs.

Reaching Cooper's, Frank rode into the runway and turned the bay over to a hostler who ambled lazily out of the shadows in the rear of the structure to meet him. Giving specific instructions as to how he wanted the horse cared for, he turned back to the doorway.

"You be a-wanting him again today?"

The hostler's question halted Bratton. Brushing his hat to the back of his head, he considered while the clean smell of fresh hay filled his nostrils.

"Not till dark—maybe not even then," he replied. "Could be I'll stay overnight. Haven't made up my mind."

"Well, seeing as how you ain't for sure, I'll get him fixed up and have him ready anytime after an hour or so," the stableman said in a resigned tone and, taking the gelding's head stall in his hand, led him off down the runway.

Frank returned to the street, turned left, and made his

55

way to the saloon he'd noticed earlier. It was small, poorly lighted, and patronized at that moment by only two men standing at the end of a short bar. There were no tables, chairs, or women to be seen, and Bratton guessed that the saloon was strictly for those looking to drink.

"What'll it be?" the barkeeper, a short, heavyset man with a full, drooping mustache asked, forsaking his two customers.

"Whiskey—and leave the bottle," Bratton said.

The barkeep quickly complied and, ignoring the silver dollar Frank laid on the counter, retraced his steps to the end of the counter where he started a conversation with the two patrons.

Downing a drink in a single gulp, Bratton stood motionless for a time, staring at his own reflection in the dusty mirror behind the bar, while the fiery rotgut liquor ricocheted through his system. And then abruptly he came to attention. The screen door of the saloon had swung back, and Monty Killeen stood framed in its rectangle. Standing just behind him was Augie Vinson and the girl, Becky.

"Bratton!" Monty called out in a hard, sharp tone as he eased slowly into the room. "Turn around! I'm going to blow your damned head off!"

* * *

Deputy Marshal Harry Locke's luck had been all bad that evening when he returned to Charlie's Place in hope of finding someone who had seen Frank Bratton leave the settlement. No one in the saloon escaped the lawman's interrogation, but the results of his careful questioning were discouraging. No one had seen or heard anything; yes, they had been told about the killing

56

of Jace Madden, but that was all.

Locke had accepted the replies stoically. At times like these a lawman usually had but a small measure of luck prying information out of anyone who might have been a witness to a crime or was remotely associated with it. And as was his way, Locke did not allow failure to discourage him. The disgrace and humiliation of letting Bratton get away from him was a stigma he could not bear, and he vowed to spend every moment from then on rectifying the lapse.

Leaving the saloon with word that he'd be at the hotel if anyone just happened to remember something, he continued to make the rounds of the settlement, questioning even Charlie Thorne, Amos Slaughter, and Prentice Axtel on the possibility that Bratton may have dropped a word or two as to where he planned to go.

Around midmorning, with Frank Bratton now at least twelve hours ahead of him, Locke returned to the hotel's restaurant and ordered a breakfast of steak, eggs, and coffee. Fortified by the food, he would then go on to El Paso and talk to folks along the path Bratton likely would have taken as he made his way into the town. It would be a long, tedious job, and by the time he was finished, assuming he had no better luck than he'd had in the settlement of Charlie's Place, another half-day and he would be down the river. By then, Frank Bratton would have a full day's lead on him, should the gambler be on the trail and not holed up in El Paso or across the Rio in Juarez.

"Marshal—"

Locke came about in his chair. It was Coaley, the stable owner.

"Yeh? You got something to say?"

"Reckon I have, Marshal. One of the gals over at the

57

saloon asked me to tell you this. Said she would herself, only the jasper she was with told her he'd beat her up good if she opened her mouth."

"Tell me what?" Locke demanded impatiently. "It got something to do with Bratton?"

"Expect so. She was on the saloon landing with this here fellow—he's a married man living right here in town, so she couldn't say his name—anyway, she claims she seen that killer ride by."

Harry Locke had now turned fully around. His eyes were bright and his features taut. "How'd she know it was Bratton?"

"Said she'd had a couple of drinks with him earlier. In the afternoon."

"She describe him?"

"Yeah, best she could. Was dark. Said he was wearing a light-colored hat and a red shirt. Could tell that much. And his horse was a bay."

"That was Bratton, all right," Locke said with deep satisfaction as he came to his feet. "Which way was he heading?"

"Toward the river," Coaley said. "My guess is he took the road north."

"Maybe," the lawman said as he laid a coin on the table for the meal and moved to the door. "And maybe not."

"What's that mean? If he—"

"If Bratton saw that woman and her friend on the landing and figured they'd seen him, he'd be smart enough to make a show of heading north, and then, when he was out of sight, double back to El Paso."

Coaley, at the lawman's heels when they came out into the morning sunshine, clawed at his stubble of beard. "Then what'll you do, Marshal? You can't just—

"

"Aim to do some asking along the El Paso road. If nobody has seen Bratton, then it's a pretty sure bet he rode north. I'm obliged to you, Coaley. And tell that woman I'm obliged to her. Getting folks to speak up is mighty hard to do."

"I'll tell her, Marshal. Good luck."

Locke shrugged as he crossed to his horse. "It's Bratton that's going to need some luck," he said. "Figured at first that maybe he was telling the truth about the killing, but running like he did sure changes my mind. I'll be bringing him in one way or another," the lawman said, and, mounting, swung off in the direction of the river.

CHAPTER 10

FRANK BRATTON, A PUZZLED FROWN ON HIS SUN-browned face, came about slowly. In the breathless tension that had suddenly filled the room, the scrape of his booted feet upon the rough, plank floor was abnormally loud.

"You goddam, lousy double-crosser," Monty continued in a low voice, "I'm going to—"

"You're going to hold it, mister, that's what you're going to do!" the bartender cut in, drawing attention to the double-barreled shotgun he was holding by thumping the counter lightly with it. "There ain't going to be no killing in here. Or anyplace else in this town!"

"Keep out of this!" Killeen said, snarling, but he had paused under the unwavering threat of the shotgun.

Augie Vinson had stepped up to Monty's side, and Becky was only an arm's length behind. Dressed now in men's clothing, she held a rifle in her hands. There was no sign of the rest of the gang, Frank noted. No doubt they were waiting outside at the hitch rack that fronted the saloon. Crossing his arms over his chest, Bratton considered Killeen.

"What's this all about?"

"You know damn well what it's all about!" Monty snapped.

"Well, it makes no difference what it is that's chawing on you jaspers," the bartender said. "You ain't settling your fusses in here. That's why I keep old Betsy here real handy." He finished, waggling the long, barreled weapon.

"And we don't want you out in the street shooting up things, either," one of the two men at the bar added, moving in behind the counter to stand beside the saloon man. "We've got us a nice quiet little town here, and we're not going to have you shooters riding in here and spoiling things."

"There won't be no shooting far as I'm concerned," Bratton said.

"You trying to weasel out of settling up with me?" Killeen demanded, his face flushed with anger. "You're not—"

"Nothing I know of to weasel out of, even if I was of a mind," Bratton replied coolly. "Let's quit the waltzing around. What's got you all riled up?"

"You pulling the stunt you did—double-crossing us, that's what! You got Sid killed. Kurt Zeller, too."

Bratton drew up in surprise. "What the hell are you talking about? I ain't seen either one of them."

"You rode right over to Flatrock and warned that station agent friend of yours that we were aiming to rob the place. They were waiting for us."

60

Bratton shook his head. "Wasn't me, Monty. Gillberg maybe was a friend of mine, but so are you, and so are the rest of the boys. I wouldn't cross you up."

"If it wasn't you, then who the hell was it?" Augie Vinson asked, his voice harsh. "You was the only one outside our own bunch that knew what we aimed to do."

"Can't answer that. Only know it wasn't me. I rode straight out of Turkey Springs for Cabezone, then came over the mountain to here."

"You got somebody who'll back you up on that?" Killeen pressed.

"Don't figure I need to," Bratton replied, his temper beginning to rise. "I said that's what I did—and it is."

Monty shook his head. "Not good enough for me. Like Augie said, you are the only outsider that knew what we planned to do. That puts the tag on your collar—"

"All of you—I'm done talking!" the bartender broke in as the second patron moved around behind the counter, pistol in hand, and took a place beside his friend and the saloon keeper. "I want you out of here! You," he added, bucking his head at Bratton, "there's a back door off behind me. Use it. Rest of you stay put till he's gone unless you want me to fill you with buckshot!"

Bratton did not stir. He had never been a man to walk away from trouble of any sort—up to the killing of Jace Madden—and he was already gut-sick of that. But he guessed there would be times in the life of a man who was trying to keep his gun in its holster when there was no choice.

"We'll keep these people right here for maybe five minutes," one of the townsmen backing the bartender said. "You climb on your horse and ride. If they catch up with you somewhere out on the flats, it's your problem, and it's nothing to us. We just won't stand for no hell-raising and shooting here in our town."

Bratton still did not move. He didn't fear shooting it out with Monty Killeen and Augie Vinson. He could handle them easily—and the girl didn't count at all. Unlike Jenny McCall, whom he'd taught to use both a handgun and a rifle, Becky was obviously a stranger to the weapon she was holding. Frank could tell that much by the nervous way she gripped it. Monty had brought her in for show, since he had only Augie Vinson to back his play. Dollar Smith and Jenny were evidently guarding the saloon's entrance and keeping watch over the horses, Frank guessed.

"You moving or ain't you?" the bartender demanded.

Frank shrugged and, pivoting on a heel, started for the end of the bar and the door he could see beyond it.

"You're not getting away from me, you—you damned renegade!" Killeen called after him. "I'll—"

"You best stay right where you are for a bit," the bartender warned. "Best you know we ain't got a regular lawman here, so we take care of it ourselves. If you or either of them with you tries to stop that jasper, we'll all three open up on you."

"You're asking for a lot of trouble, mister," Frank heard Vinson say. "More'n you can handle."

"I'm doubting that. Me and this old scattergun and the rest of the men here in town have took care of your kind before and we're still breathing."

Bratton reached the door, a hard grin on his face. The bartender and his two friends meant business, that was certain. In many small settlements like Buckeye, where there was no paid law officer to be found, the people themselves were the law and acted as they felt they had

62

to.

His horse was in poor condition to travel, Bratton realized as he grasped the knob and turned it to open the door. That was one more reason not to run, but if he was to renew the comfortable, easy sort of life he had been living up to the killing of Jace Madden, then he'd best move on, regardless, and avoid any kind of a shoot-out. For, despite the fact that Monty was forcing him into the fight, it would go against Frank because of his past prison record.

"You stuck there in that door?"

The bartender's angry, impatient question broke in on Frank Bratton's thoughts. Pulling back the thick panel, he stepped out into the gray day, a half-smile cracking his long mouth as he recalled what Killeen had called him. A renegade. What was that old saw about the pot calling the kettle black? It seemed—

Bratton drew up short, surprise rolling through him as the door slammed shut.

CHAPTER 11

JENNY MCCALL GLANCED AT DOLLAR SMITH. HE WAS off his horse and standing outside the saloon that Monty, Augie, and Becky had just entered in search of Frank. Dollar had felt slighted when Monty chose Augie Vinson to go inside with him to shoot it out with Frank Bratton and was still grumbling about it.

"Hell, I'm a better shooter than Augie," he kept muttering.

Jenny supposed there was a time when she would have felt the same about Becky, but any feeling she had for Monty Killeen was long since dead, and she couldn't

63

care less that he had given a rifle to the girl and told her to follow him and Augie into the saloon.

They had just reached the edge of the settlement after cutting a straight line from Flatrock when they saw Frank walk up to the saloon and enter. Monty had been half-crazy with hate and anger over the trouble they had encountered at the way station and blamed Frank from the start for the ambush—for the deaths of his brother, Sid, and Kurt Zeller. He was convinced that Bratton, instead of riding north as he said he would, had ridden east to Flatrock and warned his friend, the station agent, of the impending robbery.

Jenny had no idea whether Frank had done as Monty figured or not, but she doubted it. Frank Bratton was always a man who minded his own business, and while the station agent may have been a friend, she was fairly certain that he would have considered the robbery none of his affair. That was the code he and most men like him lived by; they were always ready and willing to step in and help if called upon, but a man was responsible to himself and stood on his own two feet against whatever came his way.

"That damn bartender ain't letting Monty do nothing," Jenny heard Dollar say. "He's got a scattergun, and he's pointing it at Monty and Augie."

"What's Frank doing?"

"Who? Oh, you're meaning Bratton. Just standing there with his arms crossed—calm as you please."

That would be Frank, all right. Always so cool, so completely sure of himself. Jenny was not surprised that Monty had tried hard to get Bratton to join in on the robbery. He knew Frank's capabilities, and like as not, had he been in on the robbery, matters would not have gone so badly. On such occasions Frank had been the

64

one to work out a foolproof plan—a strategy that invariably resulted in the success of the undertaking.

The Flatrock holdup had been a fiasco. Not only were Sid and Zeller killed, but the station agent and three of the men with him had been shot down. And then, to top it off, there was only fifteen thousand dollars or so in the safe instead of the fifty that Monty had claimed there would be—a revelation that had further infuriated him.

"Not worth riding here for," he'd declared, dumping the sacks of currency and coins into a pocket of his saddlebags. "And it sure'n hell's not worth Sid or Kurt." Monty had paused there and looked out across the flats to the north, his jaw set hard and his eyes burning. "But I'll make Frank Bratton pay for their lives—and pay plenty—if it's the last thing I ever do!"

Jenny remembered that Augie Vinson had then said, "What makes you figure Frank would have done that to us? He was always mighty square."

"He's changed," Monty had replied. "He's not the same Frank Bratton that used to ride with us. Nowadays he's as straight-laced as a Shaker."

"Still kind of hard to think he'd cross us up like that."

"Well, I ain't surprised none," Dollar Smith had said. "I never did cotton to him. Always made out he was too good for the likes of us."

Dollar, dull of mind and quick to follow the lead of someone else, had simply felt it necessary to make a comment, Jenny had thought as they headed straight for Buckeye, where Monty believed he might overtake, or perhaps intercept, Bratton. Augie had expressed his opinion, and Dollar felt compelled to do likewise. But in the days when Frank was one of the bunch, she recalled that he'd been kind to the slow-witted Smith and had helped him many times.

65

Jenny stirred in her saddle, glancing up and down the street. Two women were on the landing of the general store in conversation with a man who was probably the storekeeper. Other than those three, there were no further signs of life. Buckeye was a real quiet town, she thought, and then remembered what Frank would have termed it. Dead.

He would be right, but Jenny reckoned she wouldn't have minded living with Frank in a place like Buckeye. He could have held down a job as a lawman, and together they could make a nice home for themselves. Or, if Frank had wanted to be a gambler—which was now apparently his full-time job—he could have worked out of one of the saloons. They could have enjoyed a good life.

That's how it could have been if she hadn't been such a fool. Right then, at that very moment, she and Frank Bratton would still be together if she hadn't allowed Monty to move in on her like he had. She had come to realize a long time ago that it wasn't so much her that Monty wanted as it was his need to take her away from Frank, to prove that he was a better man. That was the worst part, knowing Monty needed to one-up Frank more than he needed her.

"I'm a-wondering," Dollar Smith said, turning to her.

His bearded features were slack from the liquor he'd drunk on the ride from Flatrock, and there was a bloodstain on his shirt from a minor wound he had sustained.

"Wondering what?" Jenny said, tired of the saddle and sliding to the ground.

She, too, now wore men's clothing—cast-offs from Augie Vinson and Kurt Zeller who were nearer her size. The shirt, however, had once belonged to Bratton.

66

"About me and you. Was watching Becky in there backing up Monty real good. Was figuring me and you could be like them—you backing me, I mean."

"I don't think so, Dollar. You—"

"It ain't no big job holding up a store or a stagecoach," Dollar said, scrubbing the back of his neck with a clenched fist. "Maybe I could even scare up a couple of boys to ride with us, and we could have our own bunch."

"Might be hard to do," Jenny said, striving to discourage the man. "What about Monty? He'd—"

"I ain't going to worry none about him and you're needing somebody to look after you now that Sid's dead. I—I could sure do that, Jenny, and I'd be real good to you."

"I know you would, Dollar," Jenny said kindly. "But let's not talk about it now. Not with Monty and Augie in that saloon maybe about to get themselves killed."

But maybe it would be Frank Bratton who got shot down. The odds were two to one against him. Three to one, if you counted Becky. Strangely it had not occurred to Jenny that Frank might die. Somehow she'd just taken it for granted that he would come out of any sort of situation alive. He always had, and that fact had filled her with a conviction that he always would.

It could be different this time, and evidently things were not going right, which would account for the amount of time that Monty and the others were spending in the saloon. Jenny tried to puzzle it out; could it be that Frank had the upper hand? Or was it that Monty and Augie Vinson had him backed into a corner and were taunting him before they opened up with their weapons? Surely they weren't all still standing there facing each other and doing nothing, as Dollar had earlier reported.

67

Jenny felt a stir of fear. Frank might need help this time. She couldn't just stand by, if he did, and let him face death without trying to do something about it. She owed Frank Bratton that much.

Stepping away from her horse, she crossed to where Dollar Smith stood. He had turned back to the doorway of the saloon and again had his attention on the confrontation taking place inside. Moving up beside him, Jenny looked beyond the man's thick shoulder into the shadowy room.

Frank Bratton, back to the bar, arms crossed and hat pushed to the back of his head, was facing Monty, Augie Vinson, and Becky. His dark, chiseled features were cold and expressionless. Three men stood to his right behind a short counter that served as a bar. One, the bartender, identifiable by his dirty white apron, had a shotgun leveled at Monty and the pair with him. The other two men had drawn their six-guns and were holding their weapons ready for immediate use.

"We'll keep these people right here for maybe five minutes," one of the men next to the bartender said. "You climb on your horse and ride—"

There was more, but Jenny paid no mind to the words. The bartender and the townsmen were making it possible for Frank to escape. Breathless, she waited to see what Bratton would do. Five minutes? He'd not have time to get to his horse, probably stripped of gear and stabled, and make a run for it. And, she wasn't sure the bartender and the townsmen could hold Monty and the others for the full five minutes. The way Killeen was feeling about Frank could cause him to ignore any outside threat. He might take his chances with the bartender and the two men and do as his hate dictated. It was up to her to help Bratton, and maybe, if it worked

68

out, she and Frank might get together again.

"Dollar," she said quietly, laying a hand on Smith's arm, "I think you'd best go in there and help Monty. That bartender's got him buffaloed."

Dollar turned his dull, puzzled face to her. "You reckon I ought?"

Jenny nodded. "He can use your gun and you are the best shot. You told me so."

"But Monty said for me to watch the horses. All that money's in the saddlebags on his sorrel. He won't—"

"I'll watch for you, and if Monty says anything mean to you about it, you can tell him it was my idea. All right?"

Dollar grinned. "It sure is," he said, drawing his gun.

"Now, you slip in there real quiet," Jenny warned. "Don't make any noise or you might start the shooting before you can get set."

"Real quiet," Dollar echoed, and moved cautiously toward the doorway.

Jenny waited until he had entered and was no longer to be seen. Then, wheeling, she crossed to the nearest horse. Vinson's. Since Frank wouldn't have time to get his own mount, she would provide him with one. Taking up the reins, Jenny started to turn away, and then, on second thought, lifted the saddlebags from Monty Killeen's sorrel and hung them over her shoulder.

Hurrying, she led Vinson's bay to where her horse waited and, slinging Killeen's fancy, tooled-leather pouches across her saddle, mounted, and with Augie Vinson's horse in tow, circled the saloon to its rear. When Frank came out, she would be waiting for him.

CHAPTER 12

FRANK BRATTON SWORE SOFTLY. JENNY MCCALL, astride her black mare, was waiting at the edge of the saloon's landing. In her left hand she held the reins of another horse—just whose he had no idea—but it was clear that she had brought it so he could make a quick getaway.

"Hurry!"

At her urgent prompting Bratton crossed the narrow porch, stepped down, and, moving quickly, mounted the horse.

"Five minutes isn't much time," Jenny said. "We've got to get out of town fast!"

Bratton gave the woman a brief, questioning look as they cut the horses about. He was finding it hard to understand why she was there waiting to help him.

"Which way had we best go?" she asked as they rushed out of the yard.

"Up the mountain," he replied, and spurred the bay he was riding into a gallop.

They reached the edge of town, curved in behind an empty building, and pointed their horses for the foot of the mountain, no more than a hundred yards distant. Bratton threw a glance over his shoulder when he reached the slope.

"Are they coming?" Jenny asked.

"Not yet," Frank said grimly, "but they'll be along— and plenty soon."

The horses slowed as they began the climb. Bratton had no plan for eluding Monty Killeen and his bunch. He reckoned that the only thing to do was to get a fair distance up on the mountain, find a place to pull off, and hide.

Killeen would turn immediately to the sprawling formation of Apache Mountain, knowing it was the only area that would offer any cover. It shouldn't be hard to keep out of his and the other two men's ways when they started searching.

"Whose horse is this?" he asked as the bay clattered noisily over a stretch of flinty gravel.

"Vinson's," Jenny replied. She was unusually quiet, Frank noted, probably because he had greeted her appearance with little more than frowning surprise.

"Obliged to you for your help," he said, hoping to make amends. "I'd never made it out of that stable if I'd gone for my horse."

"I guessed that was what you'd be up against."

Bratton nodded, veering his horse now to the left, where he could follow a rocky arroyo that would further conceal their trail should Monty and the others resort to tracking them. "Was a mite surprised seeing you there," he said.

Jenny's shoulders lifted and fell. They were now riding side by side and little more than an arm's length apart. "Why?" she said. "You saw Becky, and I knew you'd figure out how things were between Monty and me."

"Had an idea—but you're still with him."

"Was waiting for a chance to leave. Monty said something about going to Denver after Flatrock. I was planning to do it then."

"Yeh, I recollect your saying you had some relatives there."

She glanced at him and smiled. "You remembered that after so long a time! Yes, that's the main reason I was waiting. I'd have a place to live until I could find work. Frank, I—"

Jenny broke off suddenly as the weary mare stumbled and went to her knees. When the horse started to fall, Bratton reached out quickly and caught the woman by the arm, saving her from being pitched from her saddle. The mare recovered, no worse for the near accident, and they moved on, slicing up the side of the mountain at a long tangent.

"My turn to thank you," Jenny said.

He shook his head. "No need. You started to say something?"

Jenny squared her shoulders and stared straight ahead. "I—I just wanted to say this . . . to tell you that I made a mistake back there three years or so ago. I'm sorry. I've regretted it a hundred times over."

Bratton was silent for a time, as if searching for the words to make a proper answer. Finally, "I reckon we all make mistakes—it's part of living," he said, and added, "I've made some dandies myself—one only a couple of days back."

"You mean whatever it is that's got a U.S. marshal trailing you?"

"Yeh, that's it. I clubbed a cardsharp with my gun. Didn't mean to kill him, but I did. Caught him cheating. Rest of the men in the game didn't see it, and the fellow running the place—I figure he was working with the tinhorn—wouldn't own up to anything."

"Did the marshal arrest you?"

Frank nodded. "Was taking me in, but I got away. Couldn't make myself settle for waiting while he puzzled things out. I've already spent too much time behind bars. The marshal—name's Harry Locke—is somewhere on my trail now—not sure where or how close."

The horses slowed as a porcupine, quills bristling, ambled unchallenged across the trail ahead of them. Above, the sky was still overcast with dark clouds, and the promise of more rain was in the cool air.

"What do you plan to do? I know it's not hard to shake a regular lawman, but a U.S. marshal—"

"I'm headed for my folks' place up in the top corner of the Texas panhandle. I don't think Locke knows about my family, and I figure to lay low there for a spell. Anyway, I expect I've sidetracked the marshal, sent him on north. I'm hoping so, anyway."

Jenny made no reply as the trail narrowed and she once again dropped in behind Bratton. He was silent, also, and after a time drew the bay he was riding to a halt. They had reached a fairly wide saddle that offered a good view of the lower half of the mountain and the country below.

Buckeye was a soft-edged scatter of buildings in the morning's muted light. Smoke streamers were rising from several of the buildings, and a solitary rider moved slowly east from the settlement. Bratton studied him for a few moments, wondering if it might be Harry Locke. He finally concluded that it wouldn't be.

"We'd best be heading back for town," he said then, a plan beginning to shape up in his mind.

Jenny, off to one side a bit, looked at him in surprise and alarm. "But what about Monty and the others? Won't they be watching?"

"I figure Monty's on the mountain looking for us. Knows we're up here somewhere. What he don't know is where we'll head for."

"We?" Jenny repeated hesitantly.

Bratton nodded, frowned. "Hell, you don't think I'd ride off and leave you for Monty to find, do you? Was a big favor you did me."

"I don't want you to feel that way," Jenny said, shaking her head. "What I was thinking about is that we ought to split up. You'll do a lot better without me tagging along, holding you back."

Frank said nothing but continued to stare off down the mountain to the long, rolling flats below. Monty Killeen and the others would be on the slope somewhere. They would have spread out, Becky likely included, and would be slowly climbing the mountainside searching for a glimpse of him and Jenny McCall. They would also be on the lookout for hoofprints of their horses; the rain-softened soil would leave definite proof of their passage.

"I want to get my horse and gear," Bratton said after a time. "Feel better on him—and we'll be needing the grub in my grub sack."

"That's the second time you've said 'we,'" Jenny commented, a wistful note in her voice. "Frank, do you really want me to go with you?"

"Sure. Like I said, I can't leave you up here for Killeen and his bunch to find. Just could be that our best chance now is to head north for Denver. Monty knows I was figuring on going to my folks' place. When he doesn't find me up here, he'll probably light out for there."

Jenny's expression changed, became sad and downcast, as if she had expected a different reply. But a few moments later her head lifted and she gave him a tight smile.

"You could run into that marshal if you ride north. Why not turn around, go back to the place along the border where you killed that cardsharp? With the marshal not around maybe you could clear yourself of

74

the murder charge."

Bratton had given that idea some thought. It had merit, all right, except where the two overly eager Texas Rangers were concerned. He figured he'd have to deal with them when he returned, as he was planning to do, but if he waited, their zeal might dull and perhaps they'd listen to reason.

"That's what I've got in mind to do, only later. There's a couple of Texas Rangers there now, just hoping to get their hands on me," he said, and explained their part in his arrest and escape. "Sure would suit me fine, though. This running sort of rubs me raw."

Jenny was quiet for a long breath, then, "Would you have killed Monty back there if that bartender hadn't butted in?"

Frank shook his head. "I've quit using my gun. Had my fill of being on the wrong side of the law."

"Monty would have shot you, and so would Augie and Dollar—"

"Was thinking the same thing while I was standing there, before the bartender horned in. Not sure what I would've done. I don't think I would've just waited and let them fill me full of holes."

"You'll have to use your gun when you meet them again, whether you want to or not," Jenny said. "Monty won't quit till he has it out with you."

"No, I reckon he won't," Bratton said. "Let's go on down the mountain so's I can get my horse and gear. Expect Monty and them are pretty well up the slope by now."

CHAPTER 13

RAIN, ACCOMPANIED BY AN OCCASIONAL FLASH OF lightning and a rumble of thunder, began to fall shortly after they started the descent. It progressed steadily from a sprinkle to a drizzle, and Bratton realized that it would not soon let up. He pulled in under a pine and waited while Jenny separated her poncho from the blanket roll behind the cantle of her saddle and drew it on. He noted that it was the same poncho he'd made for her years ago, from a canvas square. Augie Vinson's gear did not hold a rain garment, and his own was with his horse in the stable. Shrugging, he resigned himself to getting wet.

With Jenny now protected from the increasing rain, they resumed their descent, swinging well to the south to prevent any accidental encounter with Monty Killeen or one of his party. They would be at least three-quarters of the way up the mountain by that time, Bratton figured, and while there was only a small chance that Jenny and he would run into them, Frank was unwilling to take any risks.

They reached the bottom of the slope, now wet and glistening from the drizzle, and drew up beneath a fair-size oak. Buckeye lay to the left of them, its lone main street deserted in the slanting rain. Frank spent several minutes studying the mountainside behind them, making certain Monty and his party were not in sight and then fixing the location of the livery stable in mind. He beckoned to Jenny and together they moved out.

"Got to make this quick," he said, keeping close to the dripping brush as they rode toward the sprawling structure. "This rain might turn Monty back, make him decide to wait."

"Doubt it," Jenny said. "Way he feels, I don't think anything will stop him from hunting you down."

Bratton shrugged. He was wet to the skin and in poor humor. "His choice," he murmured.

They reached the stable, riding to its entrance from its windowless, blind side. Working around to the rear of the building, he saw that the door was still open and quietly pulled up and to a stop. At once Jenny drew in to his side.

"What is it? What's the matter?"

"Just came to me that Monty might figure I'd come back for my horse and have somebody waiting for me."

"Hadn't thought of that," Jenny said, "but it's a good bet."

Frank said nothing. Dismounting, he handed the reins to the woman and turned toward the door.

"Anything goes wrong, you ride out of here fast. Monty'll feel the same about you now as he does me."

Jenny nodded and, smiling down at him, said, "You'll be back—I'm not worried about it."

Bratton grinned and shook his head at her declaration of confidence. Moving on, he entered the opening in the rear of the barn. He continued, bending low, and crossed the open area that lay at the beginning of the stable's runway. He halted in the deep shadows thrown by the wall of the first stall.

He had no idea where his horse would be, so finding the bay gelding would mean going up the runway and looking into each stall. His gear would be in the same compartment, which would help. If he could locate the bay quickly and slip into the stall with him, there was a good chance that he could throw his gear into place and, with a bit of good luck, lead the horse out the back

77

doorway without anyone noticing him.

The drumming of the rain on the roof of the livery stable was loud and should mask most of the noise he might make, Bratton realized, so it actually came down to not being seen. He'd need to be careful of that, but the darkness of the rain-filled day and the shadows in the barn would help him.

Pulling away from the wall, Frank headed into the runway. Lightning flashed, filling the stable with an eerie glow as thunder rumbled overhead. He paused, hearing the restless movements of the nervous horses, which could bring the hostler—and anyone else who might be in the stable—out to quiet the animals, but after several moments had passed and no one had appeared, Bratton pressed on.

The first stall was empty. He hurried on, the thought that Monty Killeen and the others, forced to give up the search for him and Jenny McCall and return to Buckeye, filling him with a taut urgency. The next compartment contained a white, and the succeeding two were vacant. Bratton halted. He was almost halfway along the line of stalls, and still no sign of his horse. Could Killeen, suspecting that he would be coming for the big gelding, have taken the bay and hidden him somewhere?

Frank considered the idea and decided that Killeen, knowing he already had a horse under him, would see little reason to do so. The bay must simply be in one of the front stalls—those that were opposite the feed and tack room and the stableman's office. He swore silently. If that proved true, his chances for getting the gelding and his gear without being seen would be about as good as filling an inside straight.

Lightning again lit up the stable, and thunder once more rattled the loose boards. Bratton bent low, moving on. He hadn't forgotten the possibility that Killeen had left Vinson or Dollar Smith to watch over his horse, but so far there had been no sign of either man, which was of little comfort. If Monty had stationed one of the two men in the stable, he would no doubt be hiding near the gelding. He gained the next stall and peered cautiously around the wall into it.

A tight grin pulled at his lips. The bay, slack-hipped and head down, was there. Checking the runway and finding it clear, Bratton glanced to the open doorway of the office a stride or two farther on. He could see no one anywhere. At once he slipped into the stall and, laying a quieting hand on the animal, pulled the saddle blanket from the wall and laid it across the bay's back. Then, careful that no metal jingled, Frank lifted his saddle, set it in place, and drew the cinch tight.

Hesitating, he glanced toward the office doorway. So far he had roused no one. Stepping quickly to the head of the bay, he slipped on and secured the bridle. With his hand on the head stall, Bratton turned again to the office doorway. Still no sign of a hostler or any of Killeen's partners. His luck was running good. Too good, perhaps. It seemed he should have heard someone moving around—or smelled tobacco smoke but there had been nothing, not the slightest thing that would indicate someone other than himself was in the building, and the quiet aroused his suspicion.

He remained motionless for a long minute, listening to the rain hammering on the roof, the roll of thunder that followed each flash of lightning, and finally, giving in, shrugged. He reckoned his nerves were too tight; maybe he was just looking for something to go wrong. His luck had been good so far, and there was no reason to believe that it was not still holding.

One hand on the bay's flank, the other grasping the bridle, Bratton began to back the horse out of the stall, being careful to keep the animal clear of the narrow compartment's plank sides. When he was almost completely in the runway, an exceptionally bright flare of lightning, followed instantly by a sharp crack of thunder, shattered the comparative stillness. The uneasy gelding jerked away from Bratton and came up hard against the stanchion at the front of the stall. There was a loud thud, the creak of leather, and the rattle of metal. Frank swore and, seizing the bay's reins, started to vault onto the saddle.

"Best you hold it right there, Bratton!" a voice warned from the first stall.

Frank swore again and, turning slowly, faced Augie Vinson. The outlaw, gun leveled, moved into the center of the runway. At the same moment another man emerged from the office—the hostler and took up a stand opposite Vinson.

"Monty figured you'd do this," Augie said. "A man likes his own horse and gear."

Frank said nothing, simply watching as Vinson moved near with great care. The hostler, nervous and agitated, glanced continually toward the open doorway and the street beyond, as if expecting Monty and the others to show up, fearing the gunplay that would result.

"Now, I never said you could—" the hostler began, but Vinson waved him aside curtly.

"Keep out of this! Best thing you can do is get back there in that office and shut the door. Maybe you won't get hurt then."

The hostler bobbed his head hastily and retreated into his quarters, closing the scarred panel that separated it from the rest of the stable.

"Sort've surprised you didn't go for that iron you're wearing when you seen me," Vinson said.

Bratton shrugged. "You take me for a damn fool? You had your gun out and pointed at me."

"Was the way I wanted it. I knew better'n to go up against you without an edge. Still, you knowing what you'll be up against with Monty, I sort of figured you'd make your try."

"Haven't used my gun on a man since I got out of the pen—"

"The hell! Hear tell there is a U.S. marshal on your tail because you killed some gambler down El Paso way."

"Wasn't a shooting. Hit him alongside the head. Died from that," Frank explained.

He searched desperately for a way out of the tight he was in. No doubt Monty and the others would show up soon and he would have no chance against them even if he used his gun.

"Well, I reckon you'll be using your iron for shooting now," Vinson said, "unless you've turned coyote."

Bratton studied Vinson narrowly in the dim light. Somehow he had to make a break before Killeen and the others came—and that might call for a shoot-out with Augie, one he was not sure he could win considering the odds.

"Reckon I'll be changing my mind," he said.

Vinson frowned, brushed at his jaw. "What's that mean?"

"Way things are stacking up here, I best start using my gun again."

Vinson laughed nervously. "Hell, you ain't about to draw on me, not with me holding my gun on you—"

"I've done it before a couple of times and I'm still around. Trick of mine. Expect it'll work again."

81

Augie Vinson drew back slightly. "Well, you sure best not try something on me!" he warned. "Monty aims to take care of you himself, but if—"

The hard pound of a horse coming fast up the runway from the rear of the barn cut into Vinson's words. In the next breath of time the bay Frank had been riding—Vinson's horse—burst out of the murky shadows as it rushed for the front door of the stable. Startled, Bratton's gelding shied wildly when the fleeing animal drew alongside. The bay's hindquarters swung into Augie Vinson, knocking the outlaw backward into the empty stall.

Bratton, alert for any opportunity that would enable him to avoid a shoot-out, swung onto his horse as Vinson, cursing wildly, went down flat into the litter on the floor of the stall. Then, raking the bay with his spurs, Frank wheeled the big horse around and sent him racing down the runway for the back door of the livery barn.

CHAPTER 14

IN THE DIMNESS OF THE LIVERY BARN BRATTON SAW Jenny swing up onto her horse, still holding the strap that she had apparently used on Augie Vinson's bay to send him thundering up the runway. She rode into the driving rain outside the stable.

"Which way?" she shouted as he drew abreast.

"Mountains! Our only chance!" he answered, raising his voice to be heard.

Jenny gave him a blank, wondering look, no doubt questioning the wisdom of heading into the direction from which Monty Killeen and his party would be coming, but she said nothing.

Bratton was aware that they might meet Killeen, and keeping along the rear of the several buildings that stood in an irregular line along the street, he led the way for a long quarter of a mile north of the settlement. Then, heading down against the slashing rain, he veered west for the towering mountain. In so doing he had taken a route that put Jenny and him well above the area where Killeen and the others would be searching.

They gained the first level of the mountain's trees—piñons, junipers, and an occasional oak—and drew in close to the most promising for shelter. It offered only a minimum of protection on its lee side from the downpour, but it did enable the horses, hard-pressed to keep their footing as they hurried across the slippery grass and weeds, a chance to catch their wind while Bratton and Jenny got their bearings.

"Monty will be looking for us on this side of the hill," Frank said, drawing up beside the woman. Water ran off him in a dozen or more rivulets, and his exposed skin glistened wetly. "Expect we'd be smart to work our way across to the other side."

Jenny signified her agreement and pointed to the poncho tied to his saddle as a vivid, blue flash of lightning lit up the area with blinding intensity.

Thunder crashed, and when it had ended, Bratton shook his head. "No time to put it on—and I sure can't get any wetter," he said, raking the reluctant bay with his spurs and starting him up the unstable slope.

Jenny angled in close behind. It was dark in the trees although it was nearing midday, but the dense growth on the mountain and the dark, rain-filled sky laid a heavy gray shroud over everything. It seemed closer to night than noon.

They rode on, Bratton picking a trail through the pines and other growth as best he could. The constant, stinging rain, which showed no signs of letting up, limited his vision, and several times he had to veer off course to avoid a gully, running fast and deep with water from the mountain's higher levels, or to avoid a tree that the wind had toppled.

The horses were having a hard time of it as they climbed the slippery surface, and it soon became apparent to Bratton that he and Jenny would have to dismount and lead the animals. Their weight made it difficult for the gelding and the black mare to hold their footing, and the last thing Bratton wanted was to see one of the horses fall and break a leg.

"Frank . . ."

At Jenny's urgent whisper, barely audible above the noise of the storm, Bratton turned to her. She pointed off to their left, her features pale and strained in the half-light. He followed her direction, swore softly. It was Monty Killeen and his party.

Killeen, followed by Becky and Dollar Smith, was moving down slope no more than fifty feet below them. Only the thick growth and the pounding rain had prevented Jenny and him from being noticed. Slipping off his horse, Frank motioned for the woman to leave her saddle also, lowering their silhouettes and reducing the chances of detection should one of Killeen's party glance their way.

"Figured they'd be more to the south," Bratton said as Jenny, crouching, moved up to stand beside him.

"Seemed that way to me, too. We're quite a ways from where we first went up the mountain."

Frank shrugged, smiled tightly. "Monty always was one to do just what you thought he wouldn't," he said.

84

Another brilliant flash of lightning flooded the slope with an eerie glow, and again thunder rolled across the mountainside. Somewhere behind them and higher up, a rushing sound could be heard. It began to increase and become louder with each passing minute, bringing Bratton about and forcing his attention toward the crest of the mountain.

"What is it?" Jenny asked anxiously. "It sounds like a—"

"An arroyo's busted loose up there," Bratton shouted above the noise of the storm. "There's a wall of water coming down."

"You think it will come this way?"

"That's anybody's guess. Can never figure exactly where one will break out. Water keeps whipping back and forth sometimes, following old washes, other times cutting new ones."

"What can we do?"

Bratton cast a glance toward Killeen and his party, now barely visible through the gloom. They were well down the slope. Either they had not heard the booming of the rampaging flood as it surged down the mountainside, or they had chosen to ignore it.

"Keep climbing, and watching, up the slope," Bratton said. "And we best lead the horses. If we—"

Lightning instantly followed by a sharp crack of thunder cut off Bratton's words. A few yards ahead a pine tree had split in two and become a fiery torch. Both horses reared in fright, the mare almost jerking Jenny off her feet as it floundered around on the slick and muddy surface of the grade. But the woman hung on to the black's reins and managed to maintain her balance.

With the sound of the oncoming arroyo growing louder, Bratton circled past the crackling and hissing pine as darting flames continued to consume it, and struck a course more to the southwest. The raging wash was somewhere to the north, he figured, but as he had explained to Jenny, its path was utterly unpredictable.

Governed entirely by obstructing boulders, trees, gullies, and unyielding clumps of dense brush, the wild flow could break out anywhere on the slope, changing courses numberless times as it plunged to the foot of the mountain. He could only listen, watch, and hope that he would spot the descending debris-laden wall of water in time to escape its destruction.

He thought the rain seemed to be slackening as, slipping and sliding, they labored slowly on. The drops hammering against his face had less force, and it was easier to see ahead. The storm was probably about over. Like most of the summer rains that came but occasionally to the high hill country, it would strike hard, leave its mark, and move on, all within a relatively short time.

Bratton halted suddenly. The rushing arroyo's roar had pitched to a terrifying level. Frank, shielding his eyes from raindrops with a cupped hand, scoured the slope above for signs of the flood of water that he realized was now racing down upon them.

"The arroyo—where is it?" Jenny asked in alarm.

"There, over to the right!" he shouted, pointing.

Jenny looked up the slope, struggling to stay upright on the uncertain surface. Her dripping face tightened as she caught sight of the foaming avalanche. A hundred yards or so distant, the descending wall was a maelstrom of surging, muddy water carrying with it small trees, rocks, bushes, rotting stumps, logs, and other litter in its path.

Bratton glanced hurriedly up the trail. A ridge of

jutting rock appeared to offer protection should the wild flood, blocked by some immovable object, veer toward them.

"Come on!" he yelled above the alarming roar. "Let's get to that ledge ahead of us."

Jenny nodded and, fighting the mare, started up the trail a stride or two behind him. It was no more than fifty feet to the ridge, but it seemed to Bratton that it was taking hours, as the booming and crashing grew louder. But they finally reached it, and pulling in close to the ragged face of the ledge, they found not only a degree of shelter from the rain but a vantage point from which to watch the ravaging torrent as it continued its irresistible charge down the mountainside.

Gradually the noise of its descent died out, and once again the steady pelting of raindrops and the now-infrequent claps of thunder were the only sounds to be heard. Wearily, both thoroughly soaked, Bratton and Jenny resumed the climb up Apache Mountain. The rain's persistence was maddening, but Frank could only hope that they would reach the top of the mountain soon and that the storm would play itself out. Until then, he and Jenny had no choice but to endure—and survive.

He glanced back at the woman. She was clinging to the tail of his bay with one hand and clutching the reins of her mare with the other. She was as soaked and cold as he was, but she had not—and he knew she would not—complain. Jenny McCall was one hell of a woman, he recalled, one any man could be proud to ride the river with.

He wished again that Monty Killeen had not come between them. If he had not interfered, they likely would not have parted, and instead of drifting along through life as a loner, he would have had Jenny at his side. But that was the past, and a man was a fool to think it could ever be changed.

They pushed on, still leading the horses. The rain slowed, renewed, slacked off again in a succession of flurries and lulls. The day remained dark and black, and full-bellied clouds hung heavy in the sky. Bratton admitted grudgingly to himself that he'd been wrong, that there would be little relief from the storm for hours to come.

He was beginning to feel hungry and realized that Jenny probably had not eaten since early morning, or perhaps even the preceding night, and also would be in need of food. Once they gained the crest of the mountain, he'd try to find a dry place under one of the larger trees where they would be sheltered and could make camp.

He had the supply of food he'd bought in Cabezone stored away in his saddlebags and grub sack, and there ought to be enough dry wood under the trees to provide a fire. Hot coffee, some warmed-over biscuits, and dried beef would do wonders for both of them.

In the next moment a grin cracked his lips. A bit of luck was coming their way. Off to their right, a dozen yards ahead, was a cabin. Abandoned or occupied, it was what they needed.

CHAPTER 15

THE CABIN, AN ANCIENT LOG AND WOOD-SLAB AFFAIR in a state of long disuse, was deserted. Rain poured through a hole in one corner of the roof, and the two windows, once covered with scraped animal skins, were now open, and gusts of water whipped through them.

But the place offered a shelter of sorts, as did the three-sided shed in the rear where they tied the horses.

"Some better than being out there in that gully washer," Bratton said as he pulled his blanket roll and saddlebags from the bay gelding. He was trying to cheer Jenny who, he realized, was on the verge of exhaustion.

She managed a half-smile as she removed her own gear from the mare and followed him into the musty, old structure.

Except for a small cast-iron cook stove balancing on three legs in one corner, the interior of the cabin had been stripped, probably by previous transients who made firewood from the bunks, shelving, and anything else that would burn.

"Expect I can scare up a little wood somewhere. Can usually find dead limbs in the pines and piñon trees. They'll be dry. I'll scout around for some while you kind of catch your breath."

"Hadn't you better get out of those wet clothes?" Jenny said as he started for the door. She shivered in the bare room's chill.

"I will, soon as I get back," he said. "No use getting wet all over again. Maybe you'd best do some changing, yourself, while I'm gone."

Jenny nodded as Bratton pushed back the sagging door and stepped out into the steady drizzle. She picked up her blanket roll and crossed to a dry corner of the old shack.

It took Bratton a good hour to collect what he estimated was enough dry wood for their needs. Although both pine and piñon trees were plentiful, and dead limbs extending from their trunks equally abundant, many were soaked from the constant rain. But by also scratching around under the trees and clumps of mountain mahogany, oak, and thick buckbrush, he was able to accumulate a fairly good stock of firewood.

Returning to the cabin, he found Jenny in dry clothing, and food laid out to be cooked for the noon meal—salt pork, potatoes to be sliced and fried along with a red onion, bread, and a can of peaches. The coffeepot, filled with rainwater caught at one of the windows, was already on the stove.

Frank went immediately to the old iron stove and, after first examining the rusty, blackened pipe rising straight to the roof to be certain it was clear, built a fire. Almost at once the cabin began to lose its chill, and a warm cheeriness filled the room.

Leaving Jenny to the preparation of the meal, Bratton drew himself back into the far corner and changed his sodden clothing. The dry garments, combined with the heat spreading through the cabin, quickly overcame the coldness that gripped him, and he turned his attention to finding a way to block the open windows and close the door.

"Are we spending the night here?" Jenny asked, glancing up from the savory mixture she'd been stirring in the frying pan.

"Storm's not letting up any, and the horses needed some rest. Expect we'd better," he answered.

"Do you think there's any chance Monty will keep on looking for us? Maybe even find us here?"

Bratton shrugged as he hung his poncho over one of the windows. "Hard to say. My guess is, he won't."

Jenny drew back from the stove and faced him squarely, her features pale and sober in the gloom. "Frank, I want to thank you for what you did."

"Thank me for what?"

"For going to the pen after that bank robbery and not

saying anything about the rest of us."

"Was you I did it for," Bratton said. "I know what it's like for a woman in prison. They're supposed to be kept apart from the men, but it don't always work out that way. Far as Monty and the others are concerned, I figured they were on their own and could look out for themselves. Could say they missed going to the pen with me by hanging on to your shirttail."

Jenny's eyes had softened. "I want you to know how grateful I am. It cost you two years out of your life."

"Didn't seem as bad as the first time they put me behind the walls. And that time was only for a year. Was before we met. Reckon I sort of learned how to handle it," Bratton said, crossing to the opposite window and blocking it with Jenny's poncho.

"It did me a couple of favors, in fact," he continued. "Learned how to make a living playing cards while I was there. There was an old man in our cell—there were six of us packed away in it—who taught us all the fine points of poker. They'd put him away for ten years, and when he wasn't outside busting rocks, he was inside playing cards. Guess I was his best pupil because when it came time for them to turn me loose, I was beating him regularly at his own game."

"I see. What was the other favor?"

"Made a promise to myself that I'd never get on the wrong side of the law again. I'd had enough looking over my shoulder and wondering who I might run into at the next corner. I've kept that promise."

"Except for that gambler you killed down near the border .. "

He nodded. "Was an accident, one I figure to get all straightened out soon as I get the chance."

Jenny had turned back to her cooking. "Where do you

91

think that marshal is now?"

"Somewhere along the west side of the mountain—if he took the bait I left for him and headed for Colorado."

The coffee in the lard-tin coffeepot on the back of the stove began to simmer and give forth an inviting aroma that blended with the smell coming from the concoction in the frying pan.

"That marshal—maybe he won't ever give up looking for you. And he could find out from somebody where your folks live and go there."

"Figured on that. I'll just cross over the Texas line into Indian territory, lose myself there for a spell. Can even change my name."

Jenny set the coffee to one side and, laying several chunks of dry bread to warm on the round lid where the tin had been, continued stirring the mixture in the frying pan.

"Frank, I think you're forgetting about Monty," she said in a worried voice. "He'll never give up hunting you, either. He's got it in his head that it is your fault Sid and Kurt were killed. And he's going to kill you for it."

"Yeh, got that idea from him back in that saloon. I'm hoping I can get a chance to talk to him, make him understand that I didn't have anything to do with it."

"He won't listen, and it'll come down to one of two things. Either he'll kill you, or you'll kill him.

Bratton crossed slowly to the stove and, using a tin cup he'd taken earlier from his saddlebag, poured it half full of coffee. Offering a swallow of the black, steaming liquid first to Jenny, and seeing her shake her head, he took a careful sip.

"Trying hard to not let it come to that—not with him or any other man," he said after a bit.

Jenny nodded. "I know you are, that you want to stay right with the law, but I don't see how you—"

"Best I figure how to cross that bridge when I come to it," Bratton cut in. "How was it with Monty after I left?"

Jenny set the spider off to the edge of the stove top and rearranged the chunks of bread so they could heat faster. Outside the cabin, the storm appeared to be fading. Lightning now split the gray day only occasionally, and the rumbles of thunder were more distant.

"Not very good. I think I've already told you that I soon realized I'd made a bad mistake."

"Yeh, we talked about it."

"I regretted what I did, not that Monty was mean to me or anything like that, but he was just never anything like you. Then, when he took up with Becky, and Sid and the others started in on me—"

Jenny broke off, unwilling to say more. Bratton finished off his coffee and set the cup back on the edge of the stove.

"It's a damn shame bad memories always seem to stick in your mind."

She nodded. "Seems they're hardest to forget, all right, but I try to remember something my papa told me when I was a little girl at home that no matter how dark a night might be, morning would always come."

"The truth for sure," Frank said. "Smells like that grub's ready."

"It is," Jenny replied, and, taking the one tin plate she'd found in his grub sack, filled it with the stew.

"I'll use the frying pan for a plate," she said.

"Then the cup's yours." Bratton grinned, pouring it full with coffee. "I'll drink out of the can."

Adding more fuel to the fire in the stove, Bratton sat down on his bedroll. Jenny made a similar seat from her gear. Then, while Frank used the one knife and she maneuvered the only spoon, they enjoyed the simple meal. When it was over, he put on fresh coffee while Jenny rinsed the utensils they had used by holding them out in the light, but still falling, rain. Finished with their chores, they settled down to enjoy the preserved peaches and hot coffee.

Several times Bratton rose and looked out the windows and door as if to be certain there was no sign of Monty Killeen or anyone else. Later in the day, he visited the horses, giving each a portion of the grain he'd purchased in Cabezone for the bay. When he returned to the cabin, he found Jenny adding more wood to the stove.

"Our clothes are about dry," she said. "If we can keep the fire going, they should be ready to wear by morning." The woman paused, her attention on him. "Frank, did you ever think about me after we split up and you got sent away?"

His wide shoulders stirred. "Mighty hard not to."

A brightness filled her eyes, turning the blue a deeper shade. "Is there a chance for us again—to be like we were, I mean?"

He gave that thought as he studied the flicker of flames visible along the edge of the stove's firebox. A lot of wind had blown down the valley since they had parted, and the bitterness that had filled him had taken a long time to fade. But fade it had, leaving in its stead a deep wariness.

"Not sure, with things being the way they are. Got that marshal on my trail, and Monty out to gun me down, I don't know just how—"

"We wouldn't have to worry about money," Jenny said eagerly, reaching for the saddlebags she'd taken off Killeen's horse. "There's plenty right here to keep us going for a long time," she added, handing him the leather pouches.

"What's this?" he asked, frowning.

"The money Monty and the others got in the robbery at Flatrock. There's about fifteen thousand dollars there."

CHAPTER 16

"THE WHAT?" BRATTON ECHOED IN A TAUT VOICE.

Through the dimness of the room he stared at the saddlebags. His features were stiff, and as he released the buckled strap on one of the pouches, his mouth tightened into a straight line, and a frown corrugated his brow.

Reaching into the bag, he withdrew several packets of currency, thumbed them briefly, and allowing them to fall back into the pouch, gathered up a handful of the gold and silver coins. For a long minute he stared at the hard money and then, shaking his head, returned the eagles and dollars to the bag, closed it, and pushed it aside.

"It's the money from—" Jenny began, but Bratton hushed her with a wave of his hand.

"Heard what you said and I sure ain't happy about it." With U.S. Marshal Harry Locke on his trail, he certainly didn't need to be saddled with the cash from a stagecoach way-station robbery.

"I thought it would help," Jenny said dejectedly, "but I guess I've only made things worse."

Bratton nodded. "One thing for sure, it'll keep Monty and his bunch hunting for us. And if Harry Locke finds us with that money, we'll both be spending some years in the pen."

"I—I never thought about it that way. It was Monty and the others who held up the way station, not you."

"That won't make any difference to the law. And with that charge of murder hanging over me, they won't waste any time putting me away."

Bratton rose, added the last of the wood to the stove in an effort to keep the damp chill from filling the old cabin. It would be necessary to rustle up another supply before darkness fell in a couple of hours, he realized, since they would not only need fire during the night but for cooking the morning meal as well. Pausing at one of the windows, he drew the poncho covering it aside and glanced out.

"Still raining," he muttered half-aloud.

The cold drops were not coming down as hard as they once had, and there was no more lightning and thunder; that part of the storm had moved on. Likely the rain would end with the day or perhaps during the night.

He hoped it would cease earlier. It was doubly important—now that he'd learned Jenny had the robbery money in her possession—that they move on as soon as possible. He wanted to pull out immediately, but it was out of the question.

Every arroyo, wash, gully, and ravine on the mountain would be running deep with flood water. The slope would be unstable and slippery and no place for a horse. To attempt to go anywhere for the time being would be foolhardy.

"What can we do with that money?" Jenny asked when he had dropped the poncho back over the opening and turned to her.

"Got to figure out something," Bratton said. "Could return it, maybe. Do you know if the station agent there at Flatrock was killed during the robbery? Name is Nils Gill—"

"He was," Jenny broke in. "I heard Monty mention it."

Frank swore softly and, taking the empty coffee cup, poured a small amount of the black liquid into it from the can. Taking a swallow, he shook his head.

"We can forget that idea, then. If Nils was still alive, I could go to him, hand the money over, and there'd be no questions asked. He'd know I had nothing to do with taking it, and he wouldn't figure you did, either—but no use talking about it. Got to come up with something else."

Jenny sighed. She was sitting on her blanket, now unrolled and folded into a square near the stove. Her hair shone in the muted light seeping into the cabin, and her face was a pale, troubled oval.

"I wish I hadn't grabbed up that saddlebag now," she said wearily. "I didn't have to—it was on Monty's horse, not Vinson's. It just seemed like a good idea at the time."

Bratton smiled reassuringly at her. "Don't blame yourself too much. I'd probably had the same notion if I'd been in on the robbery."

"I doubt that, Frank," Jenny said. "You never were the kind to take advantage or walk off with something that wasn't purely yours. What was it somebody said about you—that you were as straight as a Shaker?"

"Seems somebody said something like that," Frank admitted, smiling.

"What I want to know is, what's a Shaker?"

97

"They're real fine people, maybe kind of overly religious, but they're as straight and honest as you'll ever find. I'm afraid Monty, or whoever it was that said that, was stretching things a mite."

"I expect it comes close to fitting you, all right," Jenny said, and added, "What do you think we ought to do next?"

"Best we figure to move out in the morning. We'll be able to ride then—unless it keeps on raining."

"Do you still aim to go to your folks' ranch?"

"It's the best thing we can do. Once we're there, we can sort things out."

"You say 'we.' Are you sure you want me to come?"

"Had it in mind right along. Why? Is there something you'd rather do on your own?"

"No, I'm just surprised that you want me around after what I did to you."

"That's a long time ago. In the past. It has nothing to do with today. . . . You had a look in my grub sack. There enough to last us for eight or nine days traveling? I'd as soon not be seen in any of the towns along the way."

"I'll make it last," Jenny said at once. "Maybe we'll run short of coffee, but if you can kill us a rabbit or two, we'll get by."

"Fine, fine," Bratton murmured, and turned to the door. "Got to scare up some more wood. Expect we're in for a cold night."

Jenny got to her feet and followed him to the cabin's entrance. "I hope Monty and the others aren't out there somewhere."

"Goes for me, too," Bratton said, and smiled. "Now you know what I mean when I say it's bad to be looking over your shoulder for somebody all the time. I've been free of that since I got out of the pen—up until I buffaloed that gambler. Things are back now like they were before they put me away."

"And now Monty's hunting for you—"

"I'm not forgetting him," Bratton said, his tone suddenly stiff. He pulled on his poncho and stepped out into the steady drizzle.

He made his way quickly to the shed where the horses were standing. Pausing there, he glanced around, Jenny's words about Monty Killeen being in the area turning him cautious. The gray, wet day limited his vision, and after seeing nothing to arouse suspicion within the distance available to him, he entered the shed.

The horses were faring only fairly well. Rain entered the shack through several places in the slanting roof, and the open fourth side allowed it to whip in with every gust of wind. Taking the last of the grain he'd bought for the bay, Bratton divided it equally between the two horses and then slacked off their saddle cinches and slipped their bridles. Loosening the horses' gear would make it easier for them to rest, and it would take only moments to ready the pair once again should it become necessary to make a quick departure.

Finished, Frank pivoted to leave and then halted. His mind was on running again, on hurrying off to avoid any sort of showdown with Monty Killeen and his friends, and it galled him. Prison had ruined him, he thought angrily; no longer was he inclined to stand up to a man and have it out. Killing Jace Madden had been an accident, and it could be said that he'd had no choice. But Monty Killeen was different. He did have a choice, and he was making his decision by riding on rather than settling the matter as he once would have done.

Life had been easy and comfortable, since his time

behind prison walls. He'd taken on new ways, and he carried a gun now, only because it was expected of him. No more looking back or being wary of the shadows or the next corner. The freedom he had before the Jace Madden business had become a luxury that he was reluctant to give up. He could, and would, square up Madden's killing with Harry Locke and the law and get that off his back. But for Monty Killeen, Frank would avoid him as long as he could, even if running from him did go against the grain.

Moving out into the drizzle, Frank searched among the trees for a new supply of dry wood. He succeeded in accumulating several armloads of smaller branches and was fortunate enough to find a dead piñon that afforded a stock of larger-size limbs. He made three trips to the cabin, hauling the wood inside and piling it against the wall where it would remain dry. It was wet, tiring work, but when he was done, he felt that the labor in the constant rain had been worth it; the cabin would now stay warm throughout the night, and there would be sufficient wood on hand to cook the morning meal.

Thoroughly wet again despite the poncho, Bratton changed back into the now fairly dry clothing that had been hanging near the stove. While he changed Jenny rebrewed the coffee, using the old grounds strengthened a bit by the addition of a small amount of fresh. Earlier, she had filled a pot of beans with water, allowing them a chance to soften considerably, and now she added a few chunks of salt pork and set the container on the stove to cook until it came time to eat.

Comfortable now in dry clothes, Frank stood for a time watching Jenny go about her duties at the stove. It was good being with her again. There had been a sort of gap, a void in his life, during the past three years or so, and he was realizing that it was because they'd been apart.

He needed Jenny, and he felt that she needed him, but considering what had happened in the past, he wondered if things could ever really be the same between them again. Jenny had voiced that question, and he had been unwilling to reply; did his reluctance indicate that deep inside him he believed it was not possible?

"Coffee's ready, if you want some—"

Jenny's voice cut into his thoughts. He moved to her and waited while she poured a small amount of the beverage into a cup for herself and then handed the lard tin to him.

"Afraid this won't be as strong as you like it, but it'll be hot," she said, smiling.

In the deepening gloom of the cabin Jenny was lovely. She had pulled her hair back to the nape of her neck, and her face had a serene, smooth look. Her eyes were soft and luminous, and from her saddlebags she had produced a cosmetic of some sort that put faint color to her cheeks. The old clothing she wore hung limp and wrinkled on her slender figure, but it did not detract from her natural beauty.

Perhaps there was a future for them, Frank thought as he sipped at the steaming coffee, but the wariness that had become a part of him refused to fade so easily. The wound inflicted when Jenny had tossed him aside for Monty Killeen lay deep. And only time would tell if it had healed.

Meanwhile they had an important task ahead. They must get to Lipscomb as fast as possible. Having the money from the Flatrock robbery had complicated things considerably, and he continually raked his brain for means of ridding themselves of it. Of course, they could somehow get it to Killeen, but matters would not end there. Monty would still seek vengeance for the death of his brother and for the wrong he believed had been committed against him, and Frank wanted no shoot-out.

No, he'd have to come up with something else, a plan that would not incriminate Jenny or him. He'd keep working on it, and maybe he could think of something while they were on the way to Lipscomb.

CHAPTER 17

"YOU TAKE CARE OF THE HORSES, I'LL FIX US A BITE TO eat," Jenny said that next morning. It was just first light and Bratton, having rebuilt the fire on the stove, was getting their gear together. "I'll see to that, too," she added.

Frank nodded and, releasing the blanket he had begun to roll, crossed to the doorway and stepped out into the cool, but clear, morning.

It had ceased raining sometime during the night, but Frank could hear the steady dripping of water from the trees. The ground, as he feared, was still unstable and slippery in places. They would need to use care with the horses, and this would slow them down, but if the sun came out strong, the dark soil would dry fast and they'd be making good time before the day was over.

Frank glanced around again as he crossed to the shed and, seeing no one, continued on his way. The horses had rested well despite the rain, and after the grain he had given them earlier, they were restless and anxious to go. Slipping their bridles back into place and pulling tight the cinches, he led the pair to the front of the cabin.

Jenny had the meal ready—fried salt pork, sliced bread fried in grease, a spoonful or two of leftover beans, and coffee. While the food was cooking she had collected her belongings and had them stashed away in her blanket roll and saddlebags and was now performing the same task for him while she waited for him to return.

They ate quickly, and afterward, Bratton carried their possessions to the horses, and he tied the blanket rolls securely behind the saddle cantles and hung the saddlebags in their customary place across the skirt. He made one change; he hooked the leather pouches containing the money stolen from the Flatrock way station over the horn of his own saddle. Should they be stopped unexpectedly by a lawman, or if they encountered Monty Killeen, he didn't want Jenny involved in any way by having the cash in her possession. Also, should they suddenly get the chance to dump the money, he wanted the leather pouches handy.

By the time he finished loading, Jenny appeared with the grub sack, ready to go. He tied the sack to his saddle as she swung up onto the mare, and then mounting, he led the way out of the clearing that fronted the cabin and toward the west side of the mountain.

"Have you changed your plans?" Jenny asked at once. "I know you intended to head east across the Staked Plain country to the panhandle, and then up to your folks' place. I wouldn't want you to go north to Denver for my sake." A note of anxiety had crept into Jenny's voice, as if she were afraid he now had that plan in mind.

"No, not figuring to do that," he replied as the bay picked his way through the dropping pines. "I'm thinking there's less chance of running into Monty if we do our traveling on this side of the mountain. Soon as

103

we cover a few miles, we'll turn east."

Jenny nodded, apparently satisfied, and for a time, as the horses walked carefully along in the coolness, avoiding the wet, glistening branches and clumps of brush when they could, she made no comment. Finally, when Bratton drew to a stop at the edge of a wash still running high with roily, silt-laden water, she turned to him.

"What about that marshal? You sidetracked him, put him on this side of the mountain. Isn't there a chance we'll run into him?"

Bratton's shoulders stirred. "A chance, sure, but I figure it's a slim one. There's no guessing where he might be—a day behind, or maybe a day ahead—all depending on when he got started after me."

Jenny listened in silence and said no more until they had located a shallow place in the wash and forded. Then, as they continued on, riding side by side, she once again faced him. Her tone was sober as she spoke.

"Frank, why wouldn't it be a good idea to find the marshal? You could turn the money over to him and explain what you plan to do about the murder charge that—"

"Doubt if I could convince Harry Locke of anything," Bratton said. "Likely it would only be the start of getting myself in deeper. Odds are he wouldn't believe what I tell him about the money. More likely he'll think I was in on the robbery—and there's nobody left at the way station who could swear that I wasn't.

"And, if we run into him here, it'll prove that he hadn't taken time to dig deep into it at Charlie's Place and find out I was telling the truth. The first thing he'd do is put me in a jail somewhere."

"I see," Jenny murmured. "Things are stacked against

you more so now than ever."

"I can clear up everything once I get back to Charlie's Place—unless I get caught with this money. It could put me right back in the pen."

"I've got you into deeper trouble with it," Jenny said bitterly. "I'm sorry, Frank. I know that's not much help, but—"

"Don't fret about it. It'll all work out," he replied, but he was only saying words meant to ease Jenny's conscience.

Frank Bratton knew well that with his past record the Flatrock robbery money could put him back behind prison walls unless he came up with a safe way to return it.

The morning wore on, bright and sunny. The cold damp gradually disappeared, and by noon, riding had become almost pleasant. They saw no other pilgrims, nor were there any signs of Monty Killeen or U.S. Deputy Marshal Harry Locke. Bratton began to feel better, and with his changing attitude, Jenny's spirits also rose.

"It'll be nice staying for a while on your folks' ranch," she said as they were making their way across a grassy meadow.

"It's more of a farm or homestead than a ranch," Frank replied. "Leastwise, it was when I was there."

"I grew up on a farm, I guess you remember that," Jenny said. "It wasn't always a happy time, but there are some things I like to remember sometimes."

"I remember having to work like hell—"

Jenny laughed, the first since they'd been back together, Bratton thought. He had almost forgotten the cheerful sound of it, so light and carefree and filled with merriment. Hearing her laugh had always brought a

105

smile to his lips.

"Yes, hard work—and plenty of it. I'll never forget that," Jenny agreed. "But there were times when the chores were done and I could go out and wander through the fields or sit by the creek where there was a strawberry patch and just dream and hope and wish. Did you ever do anything like that, Frank?"

A deer bolted suddenly from the bush bordering the meadow ahead. Horns in velvet, he held his head high, big mule ears cocked back, white tail flashing as he bounded off into the trees.

"I should've been ready for that buck," Bratton said ruefully. "We would have had enough meat to last until we got to Lipscomb, with maybe some left over."

Jenny sighed. "I know it's necessary, but it is a shame to kill them. They're so pretty, so graceful when they run. That was one of the things I didn't like about the farm—having to slaughter a calf or maybe a pig for meat now and then. Papa always said I was too tenderhearted for my own good."

"Can be a drawback, all right, if you're raising stock to eat or sell," Bratton said with a grin. "Didn't you tell me I'd need to kill a couple of rabbits if we were to have meat?"

"That's different," Jenny replied with womanly inconsistency. "That's what the Lord made rabbits for. Chickens, too. I'm not sure—"

She broke off suddenly as Bratton raised his hand for silence. They were not far above the trail that followed a course along the foot of the mountain's west slope, and at times it had been visible through the trees and brush.

"Thought I heard something—a horse, maybe."

"On the trail?"

He nodded. "Would have to be down there. Could be

106

that buck we jumped. He ran that direction. Like to think it was him, anyway."

They waited out a full five minutes, their eyes fixed on the portion of the road visible to them, but when no signs of movement or no sounds other than the scolding of a scrub jay in one of the trees came to them, they moved on.

"It must have been that deer," Frank said, but from that moment on he maintained a closer watch on the lower area.

Harry Locke could be nearby. If he'd lost time before setting out to follow, and figuring a few minor delays along the way, it was conceivable that the lawman could be on the lower trail as he rode north for Colorado. But that would be stretching possibility too far, Frank decided as he sought to wipe the idea from his mind. By then Locke would be at least a day ahead of them—or should be. That was the hell of not knowing where the marshal actually was. It wasn't the same where Monty Killeen and his bunch were concerned. They would be moving toward the Staked Plain country, intending to ride north. But Locke . . .

Bratton again raised his hand and pulled up short. They had broken out of the trees into a small clearing. A quarter of a mile below on the trail a rider had halted and was studying them through a brass telescope. It was as if he had heard them passing across the slope above and waited to determine their identity. At that moment he moved slightly, and Bratton caught the glint of metal on his vest.

Immediately Frank cut the bay sharply around and started up a steep grade for the crest of the mountain. Jenny followed instantly.

"That was the marshal." She said it as a statement of

fact rather than a question when she caught up with him.

The bay and the black were taking the climb in short lunges, and for several moments Bratton did not answer, occupied in keeping the big gelding on his feet while hanging on to loose gear slapping around the saddle.

"That was him," he said when they had reached a ledge on level ground that permitted the heaving, straining horses to regain their breath. "Thought it looked like him, then I saw the sun flash against his star."

"He had a telescope. He knows it was you," Jenny said worriedly.

"Means we'll have to change the way we're heading, strike out east across the mountain. Maybe we can lose him before we get to the plains."

Jenny said nothing, but as Bratton swung the bay hard right again to continue the uphill climb, she rode in close behind him. They reached the crest an hour or so later, following a slanting course rather than continuing on a straight line to save the horses as much as possible.

Once on the summit of Apache Mountain, Frank put their mounts to as fast a pace as the downgrade would permit. He was taking little care in making their passage quiet. Locke would find climbing the slope a slow process, and it would be some time before he would reach the top where he would be in position to hear them.

They continued on at a good rate, and shortly, through the trees, they could see the plains below, stretching out in three directions in a seemingly endless, barren flat.

"We can't start across that," Jenny said. "We'll be out in the open. The marshal will see us for sure."

"Not what I'm aiming to do," Bratton said. "We'll

stay on the slope of the mountain where we've got cover for as long as we can. If Locke spots us, we'll try something else—fool him somehow or try to lose him. Right now, best thing we can do is get clear down to the bottom of the mountain."

They rode on, now angling more directly toward the foot of the slope. They could halt, Frank reasoned, until they caught sight of the lawman, and then make their move accordingly. And, waiting a bit would help the horses. Both were still blowing hard from the steep climb and the now equally precipitous descent.

"There's the bottom," he announced, relief in his voice.

The foot of the mountain was only a dozen yards away. There'd be no need now to stop and let the horses breathe; they had reached the bottom where they could halt, and the animals could rest while he and Jenny waited and watched for Harry Locke. Once they saw him and determined which direction he would be taking, they could choose their next move.

"This will be a good spot," he said, drawing the bay in behind a tall clump of juniper and dismounting.

Jenny, coming off the heaving mare, nodded. "We can see the whole side of—" she began, and cut her words short as a man's voice coming from somewhere below and to their right broke the quiet of the afternoon. Bratton, jaw tightening, turned to the woman.

"That sounded like Dollar Smith to me," he said in a low whisper.

"It was," Jenny agreed.

Bratton swore softly. "Means Monty and his bunch are coming this way."

CHAPTER 18

BRATTON THREW A QUICK GLANCE UP THE SLOPE. Harry Locke should be getting near the crest or perhaps had already started down the grade. If he and Jenny didn't move quickly, they would be caught between the marshal and Monty Killeen.

"Got to get out of here fast," he murmured to Jenny, and started to lead the bay off into thicker brush.

He had covered no more than half a dozen steps when he came to a stop. Killeen and his party were nearer than he'd thought. Clearly visible to him through an opening in the underbrush, they were riding the trail that ran along the base of the mountain's east side.

"They'll be pulling away from the slope and striking out across the flat." Killeen's words were clear and distinct. He was in the lead with Becky at his side. Also abreast and close behind came Augie Vinson and Dollar Smith. "We stay in like we are—up against the brush like this—so we'll see them when they make their move."

"You damn sure they'll be heading for the *Llano*?" Vinson demanded irritably, using the common Spanish name for the Staked Plain.

"You think I'd be riding this direction if I wasn't?" Killeen snapped.

"Could be he changed his mind," Dollar ventured.

"Now why the hell would he do that? He's running from the law—told me that. Told me he was going up to where his family has a place close to the Indian territory—where he can lay low for a spell."

"Teaming up with Jenny, that could make him change his plans," Vinson argued stubbornly. "Seems I recollect that she was wanting to go to Denver. Could be they've lit out for there."

There was a long minute of quiet during which Frank and Jenny, well concealed in the brush, watched them move by no more than half a dozen yards away. Several times, as the outlaws passed, Bratton looked toward the crest of the mountain, searching for a sign of Harry Locke. He saw nothing.

He was hoping Killeen and the others would not stop for some reason but would move on faster. It was risky for Jenny and him to remain where they were for much longer. The lawman could be close by.

"Tell you what, Augie," Killeen said angrily. "If you think I'm wrong and that Bratton and the woman are going to Denver, then why the hell don't you and Dollar head on up that way?"

"It just could be a good idea," Vinson said indifferently, "but I reckon we'd all best stay together. And now that he's got the money, I ain't taking no chance . . ."

The last of Augie Vinson's words were lost as the party rode out of hearing distance. Bratton looked once again to the slope rising above them and scanned it closely with narrowed eyes. There was still no sign of Harry Locke, but that failed to reassure him. The lawman should be somewhere close by now.

"Let's move," he said tautly, going into the saddle.

"Which way? We can't keep on going—" Jenny began as she mounted the mare.

"We're heading back—south. Toward Buckeye." Frank replied. "We're caught in the middle up here. Smart thing's to go the other way, get behind Monty and the marshal, then decide what to do."

They pushed on immediately, keeping well up on the

side of the mountain so as there would be no possibility of Killeen or any member of his gang seeing them. They were also shielded from Marshal Harry Locke since the brush and trees, more dense at that level, provided an effective screen for their movements.

They made slow time, since the ground was still soft and slippery in places from the previous hard rain, but after an hour had passed, they had covered a considerable distance and were near enough to Buckeye to see smoke rising from the settlement, although the town itself was still beyond view.

"Does the marshal know where you were aiming to go?" Jenny asked as they pulled into a small clearing to rest the laboring horses.

Frank shook his head. "No, I never said anything to him about Lipscomb. And I don't think he knows my folks live up there, but I never underestimate any lawman. They've got ways of finding out things."

Dismounting, they picketed the horses on the grassy area and sat down on a log, the remains of a pine that had been struck down by lightning.

"I'm hoping he'll just keep working north since that's the direction he saw us heading."

"Most likely he'll run into Monty and the others—"

"Probably will," Bratton agreed. "Doubt if he'll get any information out of them. Monty'll want to get to us first, so he won't be telling the marshal anything."

Frank let his words die slowly. He thought he had seen movement in the brush on the opposite side of the clearing. Turning slightly for a better view, he continued to stare at the point where the brush had stirred. It couldn't possibly be Harry Locke; the lawman couldn't have gotten that close.

"Don't get no notions about that iron you're

wearing," a voice said from the depth of the undergrowth behind them. "There's three of us, and we've all got you covered."

Bratton stiffened as a man stepped out of the brush in front of him. A second appeared to his left while the one who had voiced the warning circled about well out of reach and came into view from behind.

Bratton swore deeply. It was the three hardcases he'd seen when coming across the mountain from Cabezone. The heavier and darker of the three, his clothing worn and his boots badly scarred, was eyeing Jenny hungrily.

"Would you look at what we got here!" he drawled from behind a thick beard.

"Forget the woman, Dub," said the taller of the three. He was older than his companions and wore overalls and heavy farm shoes. "Let's see what's in these here saddlebags," he continued. "Morg, have a look-see— and mister, you keep your hands up!"

The youngest of the trio, possibly seventeen or eighteen, dressed in baggy denim pants, a calico shirt, round hat, and also wearing sodbuster shoes, hurriedly crossed to the horses. He halted first at Jenny's mare, went through the pouches, and turned to face the old man.

"Ain't nothing special here, Pa. Some old clothes and the like."

"We'll take whatever's there," Pa said. "Go see what's in them bags on the bay. Must be plenty a something, there being two of them."

Morg tossed Jenny's saddlebags to the feet of the old man and moved on to where Bratton's gelding was standing. Dub, seemingly uninterested in the proceedings, had moved, pistol in hand, to where he was only an arm's length from Jenny.

113

"My, my, ain't you special!" he said, continuing to eye the woman with relish. "Pretty as a patch of columbine."

"Told you to forget her and mind what we're doing," Pa snapped harshly. "Take that jasper's gun so's he won't be getting no ideas."

Dub reluctantly pulled his attention from Jenny and, cutting in behind Frank, yanked the pistol from its holster.

"Hey, this here bag's full of money!" Morg yelled suddenly. "Clean full of paper money and silver dollars. And gold eagles! Whooee! We're sure rich now, Pa!"

The older man took an impulsive step forward at Morg's excited words, realized that Bratton had yet to be attended to, and checked himself.

"Dub!" he snarled. "Told you to mind what we're doing here! Now get some rope and tie that bird to a tree!"

Dub, moving hurriedly, as if to get the chore over with as quickly as possible, disappeared into brush and returned shortly with a coil of rope. Pushing Frank roughly up against one of the pines at the edge of the clearing, he lashed the upper half of the tall rider to it.

"Tie his hands."

Dub nodded impatiently at Pa's words and, casting another side glance at Jenny, dug into his pocket and produced a length of rawhide.

"Stick out your hands!" he ordered, and when Bratton had complied, bound Frank's wrists together.

Bratton strained at the rope when Dub had turned away. It was tight, and while his arms were free from the elbows down, his bound hands made it impossible to get where he carried a jackknife.

"He's hog-tied and hobbled now!" Dub announced,

114

and turned again to Jenny, crowding in close to Bratton.

Pa had moved to where Morg had dumped the contents of the saddlebags containing the Flatrock stage line money onto the ground. He knelt beside Morg and, brushing aside the pieces of clothing and whatever else was in the pouches, began to paw dazedly through the cash.

"Lord, I ain't never seen so much money!" he murmured in an awed tone. "Dub, come take a look!"

Dub, sweat shining on his rough features despite the coolness, shook his head and, reaching out, seized Jenny by the wrist.

"I'm going to be right busy for a spell," he called back. "You just count out my share. I'm aiming to—"

"Leave her alone!" Bratton warned in a savage voice. "You touch her and I'll—"

"You'll do what?" Dub said with a laugh. "Maybe this here little bluebird's been your woman, but she's mine now. Come on, honey," he added, jerking Jenny away from Bratton's side. "We got us some real important business to tend to."

Jenny, eyes wide with fear, lashed out at Dub's leering face with her free hand. He laughed, caught at her wrist, and, drawing it around behind her, pinned it to her back.

"That's real spunky, honey. I sure like that," he said, pushing her toward the brush at the edge of the clearing. "Now you just behave, or I'll have to get awful mean."

Bratton struggled against the rope that held him to the pine tree, tried to work loose the rawhide that held his wrists together, but to no avail. He could move his fingers and arms from the elbows down, but none of it enabled him to reach the knot in the rope.

"Frank—"

Jenny's cry was one of desperation. She was struggling to break away from Dub, fighting him every inch of the way.

"Frank!" Her cry was now more a warning than a plea for help.

Bratton, lunging against the rope, glanced up. In that same moment he saw his gun coming at him. Jenny had managed to jerk it, unnoticed, from the outlaw's belt as she fought with him and was tossing it to him, hopeful that he could somehow catch it.

The weapon struck Frank Bratton high on the chest. Instantly, he cradled his arms, trapping the .45 against his body as it began to fall. Then, allowing the weapon to continue its downward slide until it reached his bound wrists, he worked it until at last he had it in his hands. Thumbing back the hammer, he turned it on Dub. The outlaw had wrestled Jenny to the ground, was crouched over her, tearing at her clothing.

Bratton triggered the weapon, aiming as best he could to one side of Dub. Restricted as he was, he feared his bullet might hit Jenny. The outlaw yelled a curse as the bullet whipped harmlessly past him, and jerked back instinctively. Jenny, reacting fast, yanked the outlaw's pistol from its holster and bounded to her feet. Immediately Bratton swung around the weapon he was holding, to cover Pa and Morg. Startled, they had looked around when Bratton triggered his shot and seemed frozen in their actions.

"Get over there with the others!" Frank heard Jenny order Dub as she hurried to his side.

The thick-shouldered outlaw backed slowly toward his partners. All three were staring at Frank and the girl, wondering whether to rush them—a woman holding a pistol, and a man with both hands lashed together

116

gripping another.

"Knife—in my side pocket!" Bratton said urgently.

Jenny dug into the pocket, came up with the folding blades he carried, and, opening it to the largest of the cutting edges, first sliced through the rawhide binding his wrists and then the rope that pinned him to the tree. Now, with both weapons up and ready, he crossed to where the outlaws waited.

"What are you going to do to us, mister?" Morg asked in a whining voice. "You ain't going to kill us, are you? We sure didn't mean to—"

"Shut up!" the older man snapped. "We'll take whatever we've got coming to us. Everything would've worked out just fine if Dub there hadn't been so all-fired crazy for a woman."

"Get that rope," Frank said to Jenny, ignoring the men. "We'll tie them up and leave them laying here."

Jenny hastened to do as she was bid, and then, as she held the guns on the three men, Bratton bound them hand and foot and tied their neckerchiefs over their mouths.

"We've got to get out of here quick," he said, gathering the money and stowing it in the saddlebags while Jenny collected the rest of the articles scattered around. "That shot just might draw the marshal. Maybe even Monty."

Throwing the pouches over his shoulder, he started for his horse. Snatching up her own bags, Jenny hurried to the black mare, paying no attention to the muffled protests of the outlaws, who were no doubt envisioning themselves bound, gagged, and dying of starvation and thirst there in the clearing.

Bratton, in the saddle, looked off to the north, his hard-planed features set as he considered their position.

117

Then he shrugged. Forget Lipscomb. Forget going home. The way things now stacked up, he could do but one thing.

"Let's head south, back to the border," he said. "Maybe I can clean up that murder charge at Charlie's Place. If I can't, we'll duck over the line into Mexico—and forget it."

CHAPTER 19

JENNY WAS QUIET AS THEY RODE OUT OF THE CLEARING and pointed their horses toward Buckeye. A quarter of an hour later, when it was apparent that neither the marshal nor Monty Killeen was on their trail, she pulled in nearer to Bratton.

"But what about those Texas Rangers?" she asked, the possibility of trouble from them still evidently haunting her thoughts. "You said they were out to arrest you. And what about that man who owned the gambling house? You said he wouldn't help you in any way."

"The Rangers could be gone. And as far as Charlie Thorne's concerned, I'll try a few Comanche ways of making him talk. Anyway, like I said—there's always Mexico. We can ride along the border till we come to a place where the *rurales* or the *federales* haven't closed. . . . .That was mighty quick thinking back there."

"What was?"

"Your getting your hands on my gun and throwing it to me while you were fighting off that saddle bum."

"I had to do something," Jenny said, shrugging. "I'm just glad you were able to catch it."

He grinned. "Can't say that I exactly caught it. Hit me on the brisket and slid down. I managed to get my hands on it before it went clear to the ground."

"I'm thankful you did," Jenny said with a shudder. "He was a pig. . . . Were you trying to hit him when you shot? Kill him, I mean?"

Bratton looked to the sky, now showing clear blue in the later afternoon. "Only thing I was trying to do was get him away from you—and I had to be careful. Didn't want that bullet hitting you."

"I tried to get to his gun, but he had my left arm clamped under me. I was lucky your gun fell out of his belt and onto the ground where I could reach it."

"It's all over now," Frank said, noting the strain in her voice. "Can quit thinking about it."

"Aren't they liable to get loose?"

"Sure. At least one of them will manage to, and he'll cut loose the others."

"Suppose they start following us, too?"

Bratton shook his head. "That ain't likely, but they might've already put the marshal, and maybe Monty, on our trail. All depends."

"On what?"

"On whether that gunshot drew their attention and whether whoever heard it was nosy enough to ride back and see what was going on. They could all pass it up, or they could figure we had something to do with it."

"You should have killed them—all three of them!" Jenny said with unexpected vehemence.

Frank glanced at her. They were following a trail that was fairly wide, and the horses were walking abreast. Jenny's features were taut, and there was a brightness in her eyes that heightened their blue color. Life had not been easy for her, he knew, and while it could be said that she'd been many places and had seen the elephant, conversely, the encounter with the man they called Dub had unnerved her badly. She was finding it hard to erase him from her mind.

"You don't like shooting—killing, do you?" she asked after a bit.

It was a surprising question. Bratton considered it for a moment or two and then shifted on his saddle. "Never have. Guess there was a time when I wouldn't go out of my way to dodge a shoot-out, but I've sort of changed in how I look at things. I reckon that last stretch in the pen made me see things in a different light."

"Does that mean you don't ever intend to use your gun on a man again?"

Bratton kept his eyes straight ahead. They were moving across the side of Apache Mountain, fresh and cool as was always the way of the country after a cleansing rain. The foot of the slope lay a quarter of a mile below, and rolling out from there was a vast plain that extended indefinitely to the east. The pines around them stood tall and straight, like soldiers called to attention, while above, the vivid blue sky was now devoid of any threat of rain.

It was a soothing relief to be riding through the cool, dappled forest after what they had experienced, and he wished Jenny's thoughts could be more lighthearted. He watched her as he mulled over the question she'd voiced, then gave his reply.

"Can't answer that. I reckon it'll depend on what it's all about."

Jenny listened soberly, and then, twisting about on her saddle, glanced worriedly at their back trail.

"Do you think Monty, or the marshal, has found those outlaws yet?"

"Maybe," Frank said, "but if either of them did, it still wouldn't mean somebody'd be on our trail all this soon.

Be a job getting one of them to talk."

"Why?"

Bratton grinned wryly. "Well, any renegade outlaw like me sure wouldn't want to help the law," he said in a mocking tone, "and as far as lending a hand to others of their kind—that's not usually done, either. The outlaws will figure that Monty and his bunch are on their own, same as them."

"Monty will find out, and he'll know we've headed back south," Jenny said. "I know him and just what he'll do. He'll have Dollar and Augie beat it out of those men if they can't make them talk otherwise."

"Probably what they'll have to do. Can say the same for Harry Locke. If he gets an idea they know something, he'll get it out of them one way or another."

"So there's no doubt Monty or that lawman are on our trail or soon will be —"

"Can bet on it, but don't fret. We've got a good start, and we've got the upper hand."

"I—I don't understand. In what way?"

"They're chasing us. Means we can pick our own trail, same as we've got a better chance of spotting them before they do us. Right now we're holding all the high cards."

Bratton's words seemed to satisfy Jenny and relieve her worry as they rode steadily on, and soon she had brightened considerably. They would need to pull in, make camp for the night within a couple of hours, he realized. He pondered which would be the better choice—to go higher up on the mountain or to drop lower where the brush was denser.

His confidence in the safety of their position wasn't actually as strong as he had indicated to Jenny, but she had been so distraught that he felt compelled to stretch

121

the truth a bit. He was positive Harry Locke would be on their trail by now. The old marshal would miss nothing, and it was a sure bet that the lone gunshot had drawn his attention, and he had made the most of his meeting with the three saddle bums.

As to Monty Killeen, odds were that he had taken note of the gunshot, investigated, and if the three outlaws were still around, obtained his information from them and was following. That Monty would avoid the marshal was a certainty, and he would find out who got to the three saddle tramps first when he discovered who was nearest behind him and Jenny.

It proved to be Monty Killeen. Bratton and Jenny had just halted on a small, rocky plateau to breathe the horses after climbing a length of steep grade, when Frank caught a glimpse of riders well down the slope, half a mile or so to their rear. He said nothing at first to the woman; she was near exhaustion after the long day in the saddle and her trying experience with the outlaw, Dub, and he wanted to spare her as much anxiety as possible.

The trees and brush, combined with the long shadows of the closing day, made visibility poor, and. Bratton was not absolutely certain it was the Killeen gang he saw, but when four riders broke out into an open area and one of them was a woman, he became sure.

"Got to move on," he said, taking Jenny by the arm and moving to her horse. "They're coming—"

"Monty?" she asked, going into her saddle. "Where are—"

The woman didn't need to finish her question. Looking back down the slope, she saw Killeen and the others moving along the trail at a fair pace.

"Best we head up the mountain," Frank said,

swinging onto the bay. "If we can keep out of sight for another hour or so, it'll then be dark. Be no chore after that to lose them."

At once he turned the gelding toward the crest of Apache Mountain, the iron-shod hooves of the horses clattering noisily over a narrow, flinty plateau. The sound was brief but long enough to draw the outlaws' attention.

"They've seen us," Jenny said, her voice rising. Unlike her tone when she had spoken of the bearded Dub, there was no fear in it.

Bratton swore. He'd been careless, had let down his guard for only a quick moment and betrayed their position. He should have seen the rocky plateau and circled around it.

"Only thing we can do is keep climbing. They'd cut us off if we doubled back," he said tersely.

Abruptly a gunshot rang out. One of the party had brought his rifle into use. The bullet struck a boulder somewhere to their left, went singing shrilly off into space. Bratton slowed and waited until Jenny was abreast. They were following no trail, simply taking a course of least resistance as they made their way between the trees, brush, and rocks.

"Want you to keep going up," Bratton said in a quiet voice as the rifle shattered the mountainside again. "Head for that peak," he added, pointing to a bald knob thrusting out from the slope near the crest some distance away. "I'll meet you there."

Jenny frowned. "What are you going to do?"

"Take Monty and his friends on a little snipe hunt," Frank said with a grin, and before the woman could make any objections, he wheeled around and started down the grade.

123

The rifle cracked for a third time, its echo rolling endlessly along the slope. Bratton did not slow. He had no idea where the bullet had struck—below him and to the right, he thought, but he couldn't be sure. Whoever it was using the long gun was firing blind, levering bullets at flashes of motion seen only briefly through the brush and trees.

The bay continued down the slope at a good pace, but Bratton was keeping a tight rein on the big horse. He was taking no chance on him falling and injuring them both. Again the rifle spoke, three times in rapid succession. Dirt and litter spurted up ahead of Bratton. A hard smile pulled at his lips. The rifleman had gotten a good look at him that time! He slowed as a voice carried to him. The words were clear and urgent.

"They're a-heading for town!"

For town. For Buckeye. Frank hadn't realized that they were so near the settlement. At once he changed the near direct downhill course of the bay to one that angled more toward Buckeye, not visible from where he was but whose location was marked by smoke streamers twisting up into the sky.

Two more shots sounded, both bullets screaming off rocks behind him. It had worked out as he'd hoped. Not only had he drawn attention away from Jenny, but also he had strengthened Killeen's belief that he and the woman were hurrying to reach Buckeye and seek a hiding place or help from the townspeople. Making no effort to conceal himself and the bay, he moved steadily on. There were no more shots, and he reckoned he was no longer visible to the rifleman. Then, reaching a thick stand of juniper and piñon trees, he rode into it and halted.

Somewhere below, he could hear Killeen shouting.

Frank strained to make out what was being said. Killeen ordered Dollar Smith to stay on the slope and keep a close watch on the trail. "Make sure that goddam double-crossing Bratton and his thieving woman don't start doubling back," Monty called.

His instructions to Augie Vinson were pretty much the same. Augie was to hang around the foot of the mountain, also keeping his eyes open. Monty and Becky would ride on into town where they'd watch for Bratton and Jenny to arrive. Then, when darkness came, Dollar and Augie were to join them.

It couldn't be better, Bratton decided, climbing off the bay and hunkering down on his heels to wait. He heard no more of their voices although at one time, a quarter of an hour or so later, he heard a horse passing by somewhere below. It could be either Smith or Augie Vinson; there was no way of knowing which.

Or it could be Deputy Marshal Harry Locke. That realization came suddenly to Frank as he hunched there in the midst of the brushy trees. It was what a man could expect of the lawman; he had somehow discovered that Killeen and his hunch were trailing the same man he sought and was simply holding off, letting them do all the work.

Only, if Harry Locke, like Killeen, thought he was going down to Buckeye, he was badly mistaken. As soon as he could join up with Jenny he would strike south, give the settlement a wide berth, and head for Charlie's Place. And maybe Mexico.

CHAPTER 20

THE TIRED BAY CLIMBED THE SLOPE AT A LAGGING PACE but finally reached the rocky knob where Jenny was anxiously waiting.

"All that shooting. I was afraid you'd maybe—"

Frank brushed her words aside. "Just a lot of wasted ammunition," he said as he dismounted. "He never did come close to hitting me."

Jenny followed him to the ledge beneath the peak, where they both sat down. Pushing his hat to the back of his head, he said, "Got to rest my horse a bit. Then we'll move on."

"What about Monty and the others?" she asked.

"He figured we were lining out for Buckeye. They're looking for us to show up there. I think the marshal is, too."

"Then we best go on."

Bratton nodded. "We'll keep the mountain between them and us. There's a trail that crosses over—I used it before. It will put us on the west side."

"You still think the best idea is to go back to that gambling house?"

Bratton wiped the sweat off his forehead with the back of a hand. He'd worked up a bit of steam in the past half hour despite the evening coolness that was setting in on the slope.

"Still do. Monty won't wait until he tracks me down, and neither will the marshal. No matter where I go, they'll show up sooner or later, so why not go back to Charlie's Place where my trouble with the law started and try to make Thorne or maybe one of those other gamblers—Slaughter or Print Axtel—own up to the truth?"

"That would clear you with the law, but what about Monty? You talk about sooner or later, well, sooner or later you'll have to face him. And the way you feel about using a gun . . ."

He glanced at her. The flare of gold in the west that filled the sky as the day ended was on her face, highlighting her eyes and giving her skin a soft, mellow look.

"You got some idea that maybe I'm scared of going up against Monty?"

"No, not that you're afraid, but you don't seem to want to use your gun—to kill, I mean—and when you and Monty meet, it's going to be a matter of who shoots first. You won't have time to sort out what's right and what's wrong in your mind."

"Thought of that a time back," Bratton said, "and I'm not sure what'll happen. Way I see it now, I'll just have to cross that creek when I come to it. One thing I'd like to say again—we've got to get rid of that money. Chances for somebody finding it on us are getting better."

Jenny shrugged impatiently. "I wish to hell I hadn't taken it! I guess I just wanted to spite Monty—and I did have some thoughts of it being for us, that we could use it to start a new life."

"Sure be a mighty fine nest egg, all right, but if we do start over, we'd best start clean, not be worried all the time about somebody showing up and asking questions that could maybe put us behind bars."

"I know, Frank, and you're right. Have you figured out yet what to do with the money?"

"There's a sheriff in Turkey Springs. I'll hand it over to him when we go through."

Jenny frowned. "How will you explain it?"

"I'm no hand at lying, but I can say I found it along the trail, that it must have dropped off a stagecoach or somebody's saddle. I'm saying I found it because I don't want you mixed up in it at all. . . . You tired?"

Jenny smiled. "I've been tireder. I'm ready to move out whenever you are."

Bratton rose, reaching out a hand to assist her. She showed her appreciation for the courtesy in her eyes, accepted his assistance, and walked quickly to where she had tethered the black mare.

"Figured we'd keep going until early morning, then pull up and rest. Can maybe fix a bite to eat. I've got no way of knowing how long Monty and the marshal will hang around Buckeye, but I'm hoping they'll stay long enough for us to get a good start on them."

"Are you certain they'll think we've headed south?"

"Pretty sure. Monty gave Dollar Smith and Vinson orders to watch and see that we didn't double back north and they could spot us if we headed east for the Staked Plain country. About the only choice left is south, because there's nothing but open country west. Besides, those saddle tramps probably heard us talking, and they'll have told Monty or the marshal—whichever one got to them first, what we said," Bratton finished as he went to the saddle.

Jenny said, "Yes, I remember now our talking about which way to go." She had mounted and was waiting for him.

"We'll have them fooled for a while," Bratton said, "so there's nothing to fret over now." Raking the gelding lightly with his spurs, he put the big horse into motion.

They were somewhat to the left of the trail he had

followed when crossing the mountain days before, but the country was pretty much the same—plentiful trees, dense brush, and scattered rocks, none of which made riding particularly difficult.

At the beginning, as the horses climbed the remaining distance toward the mountain's crest, their pace was understandably slow, but once on the summit and starting the opposite downgrade, the animals had it much easier. Bratton kept them at it, although both Jenny and he were having trouble staying awake, until they were little more than a mile from the foot of the slope and the trail that ran along its ragged edge. Then they pulled to a halt beside a small creek that wound its way through a grassy swale.

"There's a town called Cabezone on down a ways," Frank said as they came off their saddles. "Could keep going till we got there, but I'd as soon we'd pass it up, not leave any signs of us going by."

Jenny was taking the grub sack off his saddle and reaching into one of the saddlebag pouches for the coffee tin and frying pan. He grinned, nodding his approval.

"Expect you're figuring right. We probably won't have much chance to stop and eat once we get moving. Got to keep ahead of Monty and the rest," he said. "I'll start a fire."

They ate, resting for better than two hours in the swale, and then, in the muted silver shine of the stars and moon, packed up and rode on. The sun caught them shortly before they reached Cabezone, and Bratton, precaution foremost in his mind, swung well clear of the small settlement.

They made only fair time that day, as the horses were worn and in poor condition. Bratton found it necessary

129

to pull up early and make a dry camp at the edge of a brushy arroyo. They watered the horses from canteens filled from the creek back on Apache Mountain, built a small fire—one only large enough to make coffee and warm over some beans, potatoes, and the last of the bread—and then spent the night there.

Several times during the starlit hours Frank roused and, moving off to one side, listened into the hushed, silvery night. Once he thought he heard hoofbeats on the trail a mile or so to the east, but he was not certain. Only the coyotes and the wolves appeared to be around, taking turns disturbing the quiet with their discordant howls.

The morning meal was scant—the last of the salt pork, more beans and potatoes, an onion, and weak coffee.

"Can stock up when we get to Turkey Springs," Bratton said as they loaded up and angled back for the trail.

"Is it far?" Jenny wanted to know.

"We'll make it before the day's over if nothing goes wrong."

She considered that thoughtfully. Then, "What could go wrong? Don't you think Monty and that marshal are still back in Buckeye?"

"Not much of a hand to take anything for granted, but I'm hoping they are."

Jenny sighed heavily. "I'll be glad when this is all over. I—I'm worried about you."

"You thinking about when I go up against Monty someday?"

The woman nodded and then continued boldly. "I'm praying you and I can have a life together. Not just one where we're wandering around the country, a pair of fiddle-footed people, but a couple who have a real home where they can raise a family and live decently."

Bratton listened without comment. He was staying well clear of the trail to Turkey Springs; swinging wide would consume more time, but the chances of their being seen by Killeen or Harry Locke, should they be close behind, would be far less.

"But if you're reluctant to use your gun," he heard Jenny continue, "or maybe be a mite slow doing so, I'm afraid we might not even have a future together—if that's what you want, too."

Frank maintained his silence as they pressed on, riding steadily along through the brushy swales and arroyos west of the main road. After a bit, Jenny looked off toward the plains to the east, an expression of hopelessness in her eyes, as if she were realizing the futility of her dreams. At that moment Bratton turned to her, his dark, sun-browned features set to hard lines.

"Found out a long time ago that it didn't pay to plan too far ahead. We'll decide about all those things you're wanting out of life after there's been some settling up done."

"You mean, after you've got things straight with that marshal and meet up with Monty?"

He nodded, brushed at the sweat building on his forehead. Although early, it was already getting hot. "That's about the size of it."

They rode on, encountering no one headed north from Turkey Springs or anyone bearing south from Cabezone, but as the trail was only visible to them at intervals, they could not be certain if they were the only riders making a passage.

Around noon they reached the settlement. Frank immediately veered toward the general store that stood

131

at the edge of town and drew up at the hitch rack. Pausing first to give a long, searching look northward to be certain that there was no one in sight, and being reassured, he reached into a pocket, produced a gold eagle, and handed it to Jenny.

"Stock up on what grub you figure we'll be needing," he said. "Still about two days traveling to Charlie's Place. I'll meet you back here."

"You're going to see the sheriff and turn that money over to him—"

"That's where I'm headed. Now I want you to stay right here. I don't want the law realizing you're one of the women that was mixed up in the robbery. He'll know all about what happened at Flatrock by now."

Jenny signified her understanding and began to dismount. Frank turned away and, avoiding the town's one main street, continued on, finally coming to a stop at the rack alongside one of the saloons. Securing the bay, he walked to the front corner of the building and stood there for a time until he located the sheriff's office—a short distance farther down and across the street.

Glancing down the dusty roadway, deserted on that hot midafternoon, he crossed the street and made his way to the lawman's office. An elderly man in a sweat-stained blue shirt, dark pants, and almost-new boots was sitting in a straight-backed chair, feet propped on a desk as Bratton entered the overheated office.

"How do," he greeted, glancing up.

Bratton nodded. "You the sheriff?"

"Nope, the deputy. Name's Harden. Sheriff's gone for a couple of days. Something I can—" The lawman broke off as a bell somewhere in the settlement began to toll slowly. "That's for old man Cassidy. They're

132

burying him today," he explained, and then continued, "Something I can do for you?"

Bratton took the saddlebags hung across his shoulder and dropped them onto the desk. "Came across these a ways back. Moneybags inside says it all belongs to some stage line."

Harden had come to attention. A look of suspicion sharpened his features as he unbuckled the pouch containing the money and withdrew one of the muslin sacks packed with coins and currency.

"Was stole over at the Flatrock way station," Harden said, reaching for his bandanna to mop his glistening features. "Where'd you say you got it?"

"Up along the trail. Somebody, I reckon it was the holdup man, must've lost it."

Harden continued to finger the cash, a deep frown corrugating his forehead. "Seems to me you're mighty honest to be turning it in."

Bratton stirred apathetically. "Deputy, you've been up against outlaws too long," he said dryly. "There's still a few honest folks around. However, if you're not of a mind to bother with it, I reckon I can hang on to it till I get to El Paso and turn it over to Dallas Stoudenmeyer. He—"

"Hell, ain't no need for that!" Harden cut in, voice rising sharply. "Me and the sheriff'll be right pleased to see the stage line folks get it back. Flatrock ain't far from here—that's where the robbery took place."

Frank considered Harden's words for a long breath. Frowning, he said, "Sure'd like to know for certain that the money gets back to who it belongs to."

Harden bristled, again mopped his face. "You saying maybe me and the sheriff'd just split it and not say nothing to nobody about it? Dammit, man, we've been the law here for twenty years and we ain't done nothing to be ashamed of yet!"

"I'm mighty glad to hear that," Bratton said mildly. "Reckon I could ride over to Flatrock with it myself, only I ain't going that way."

"Ain't no need for you to do that," Harden said, coming out from behind the desk. "Me and the sheriff'll see that the money gets delivered safe. Mind giving me your name so's I can tell the sheriff who it was that found this here money and brought it in? Besides, there'll maybe be a reward."

Frank shook his head. "Not looking for thanks—or any reward," he replied, avoiding an answer. "If the stage company is feeling generous, you and the sheriff split it. Hear they don't pay you fellows enough, anyway."

"Well, now, that's right kindly of you," Harden said, smiling broadly.

"My pleasure," Bratton said, and, hanging the empty saddlebags across his shoulder, turned to the doorway of the office and stepped out into the driving sunlight.

Dropping back to where he left the bay, Frank hung the pouches on his saddle, mounted, and made his way to the general store. Jenny was still inside, and climbing the steps to the landing that fronted the structure, he opened the screen door and stepped inside. Jenny turned to him, relief immediately relaxing her features.

"Did everything go all right?"

"Just the way we wanted," Bratton replied, reaching for the now well-filled grub sack.

The storekeeper, a squat, balding man with steel-rimmed spectacles, and wearing a denim bib apron over a black satin shirt and tan duck pants, bobbed happily to Frank.

"It's a pleasure to do business with your missus," he said, laying some change on the counter for Jenny. "Hope you'll come in again."

Bratton smiled briefly and, with Jenny preceding him, started for the door. "Hope so myself," he murmured as they reached the dust-clogged screen and stepped out onto the landing.

Instantly Frank Bratton came to a stop. A mixture of surprise, frustration, and anger surged through him. Standing at the foot of the steps was Deputy Marshal Harry Locke.

CHAPTER 21

EVIDENTLY IT HAD BEEN THE MARSHAL WHO HAD found the three saddle tramps first. He'd exacted from them the information he needed and had gone on to Buckeye, Bratton reckoned. Sometime later, when he and Jenny failed to show up at the settlement, Locke had ridden out to Turkey Springs, taking the shortest route possible. Frank had no way of knowing how long he'd been waiting; only briefly, he suspected.

"Give that sack to the woman and put your hands up," Locke ordered in a hard-edged, no-quarter voice, moving the gun he was holding suggestively.

Dust lay upon the lawman in a gray film. His neglected beard had grown, and his small, red-rimmed eyes were narrowed, as if he were looking into the sun.

"You hear me?" he demanded when Bratton did not comply.

Frank shrugged, passed the grub sack to Jenny, and raised his hands. Behind him the storekeeper had hurried up to the window of his shop and was watching

135

and listening avidly.

"Now, come down here."

Taking deliberate steps, Bratton crossed the landing and descended to the ankle-deep dust of the street. His features a frozen, brown mask, he faced the marshal.

"Took some figuring and riding," Locke said, satisfaction filling his voice, "but I've run you down. I damn sure aim to make you pay for putting me through what you did."

Locke's tone had risen with anger, and his eyes had taken on a sharp glint. "Ain't never lost a prisoner yet, but you come damn near spoiling my record. I don't figure to ever let something like this happen again—not with you or any other jasper!"

Bratton, a heaviness weighing on him, shook his head. "That murder charge against me is all wrong, Marshal. I was out to prove that."

"By running north? I'd maybe believe that if you'd ducked across the line into Mexico, but you took off in the other direction." The lawman paused, jerking a thumb at Jenny, who was now standing at Frank's shoulder. "Who's the woman? Don't recollect seeing her around before."

"She's a friend of mine," Bratton said non-committally. "My folks've got a place up in the top of the panhandle. Was aiming to go there and lay low for a spell, then ride back down to Charlie's Place and straighten out the trouble I'm in."

"Sure, sure," Locke said, brushing the explanation aside. "Now start walking," he added, waggling the pistol in his hand. "I'm going to stash you away in Fred Eagleton's jail and then see where the judge is."

"He's not guilty of murdering that gambler!" Jenny said in a rising voice. "Those men know it—same as you do! If you'll give him the chance, he can prove it."

"I recollect he tried. Them fellows didn't back his claim," Locke said.

"That was because they were afraid or else just didn't want to. Reason we're right here now is that he was on his way to see this Charlie Thorne and make him own up to the truth."

"Just what I had in mind to do in the first place, but he up and run away from me."

"Had no choice, Marshal," Frank said. "You or those two Rangers were dead set on locking me up—and I've had more'n enough of that."

"Well, like as not, you're in for a spell of it again, for sure. Move out."

Bratton glanced at Jenny. Her face had a stricken look, and tears mixed with the hopelessness in her eyes.

"Get yourself a room at the hotel while I see if I can work this out. If I can't, you'd best catch the stage for Denver and join your kinfolk." Frank paused, shifting his attention to Harry Locke. "It all right if I reach into my pocket? The lady's going to need some money."

The lawman thought for a moment, then nodded.

"Sure, just so you do it real slow and keep that other hand up high."

Bratton did as directed, producing several eagles and some silver, all of which he passed to Jenny.

"Don't fret about this," he said, forcing a smile. "Expect I'll be able to square things up."

"Now, I sure wouldn't bank on that, lady," Locke said, and again motioned with his weapon. "Turn around, Bratton. I aim to pull that iron of yours, then I want you to start walking—"

"What's going on here?"

Deputy Harden, boots shining in the bright sunlight,

features drawn into an angry frown, hurried up. Beyond him in the street, several men, attracted by the meeting in front of the general store, were watching from a safe distance.

Harden slowed abruptly when he recognized Locke. "Oh, why, howdy there, Marshal. I didn't know it was you. What's the tro—" He broke off when he got a full look at Bratton. "You a-wanting this fellow for something?"

Harry Locke spat into the dust. "Nothing much," he said dryly. "Only for murder and for getting loose from me while I was taking him in."

"That a fact!" Harden said in a marveling tone. "It ain't been more'n thirty minutes ago when he come to my office and turned over the money them outlaws stole from the Flatrock way station."

Locke drew up sharply. "What was that?"

"That's right, Marshal. He handed over all the cash them killers took. Said he found it up the way a piece."

The lawman studied Frank coldly for a full breath. Then, "Where'd you get that money?"

"The deputy told you. Take his word for it. I had nothing to do with that robbery, if that's what you're thinking. What I said back at Charlie's Place about going straight is the truth."

Locke scrubbed wearily at his jaw. "I'm beginning to think maybe what you claim is true," he said. "Leastwise, it's sure worth digging-into before we get the judge mixed up in it."

Bratton lowered his arms slowly. "All I'm asking is a chance to prove I killed that gambler accidently—and that he was cheating. If you'll go back to Charlie's Place with me, I figure we can make Thorne talk if we put it to him hard. Same goes for that counter-jumper and that

138

rancher."

The marshal was silent for several moments, and then weariness finally seemed to have its way with him. He holstered his gun and shrugged.

"Fair enough. We'll ride on down to Charlie's Place and have us a talk with that bunch. This time I'll find out for sure who's telling the truth. . . . You and your woman go on over to the hotel, get yourself a room. I aim to do the same. We'll ride out in the morning."

Bratton heaved a sigh of relief. At last he had Harry Locke seeing things his way. "I'm obliged to you, Marshal. Just need the chance to prove what I claim."

"Can show how much obliged you are by not trying to escape again," Locke snapped. "I'm for damn sure beat, but if you try it, I ain't in such bad shape that I won't take right out after you."

"No chance of me doing that. I want that murder charge off my back. Found out that not having the law dogging my tracks is a fine way to live. Besides," he added, taking the grub sack from Jenny, "I've got me somebody to look out for now."

Harry Locke nodded. "Well, you just keep feeling that way and you won't ever have no more trouble with me and the law. I'll meet you in the livery barn back of the hotel at first light."

"We'll be there," Jenny said, speaking up. Her voice was light, filled with happiness, and there was a sparkle in her eyes. She was every bit as weary as Bratton and Harry Locke from the long, hard ride, but the joy of hearing what Frank Bratton said about her, as well as the lawman's changed attitude, had apparently wiped the exhaustion from her body.

Wheeling, Locke moved off down the street with Deputy Harden at his side. The men who had gathered

139

to watch had disappeared, and the storekeeper no longer stood at his window of his establishment. Bratton looked down at Jenny and smiled.

"Expect we'd better do what the marshal said, but the horses come first. We'll stable them and sign in at the hotel afterwards."

Together they walked to their mounts, climbed into the saddles, and rode the short distance to the barn at the rear of the hostelry.

"Did you really mean what you said to Locke about us—about you looking out for me?"

"Sure did. And if you're needing convincing, we can scout up a preacher while we're here and have him do the job up right and for good."

The blue of Jenny McCall's eyes became even brighter. "Oh, Frank, can we?"

Bratton nodded slowly, but his attention was straight ahead on three men and a girl standing in the shadows just inside the entrance to the livery stable.

"Sure can—and will," he murmured. "Only it'll maybe have to wait a bit."

Jenny, sensing the abrupt change in him, turned her attention to the direction in which he was staring. A sigh of hopelessness escaped her lips.

"Monty!" she said in a falling voice. "He's caught up with us."

CHAPTER 22

"KEEP ON COMING, FRANK," KILLEEN SAID IN A HARD tone. "I want that money, then I'm settling up with you for Sid."

Monty and Dollar Smith both had their guns out.

140

Augie Vinson had not drawn his weapon but stood, arms folded across his chest, a bit to one side. Becky was sitting on the step leading into the office of the stable owner, showing signs of utter exhaustion.

"You didn't fool me any," Killeen continued as Bratton and Jenny halted in the stable's wide doorway. "Got to admit you damn near did. But when we spotted that lawdog chasing you, nosing around and asking questions, we just kept an eye on him. Then, when he headed south, we followed. It worked out real fine."

Bratton lifted his shoulders resignedly. He had done his best to cover his and Jenny's trail—and had failed. Likely he would have succeeded in leaving Killeen behind if Harry Locke hadn't found the saddle tramps, and then later, on a hunch, hurried on to Turkey Springs.

"You won't have to worry any about going back to the pen. I'll see to that," Monty added with a half-smile, then shifted his cold gaze to Jenny. "Aim to settle with you, too—make you sorry you ever double-crossed me. . . .Where's that money?"

In the taut, tension-filled moment that followed Killeen's question, Bratton felt Jenny's eyes upon him. He shook his head at her, warning her to silence. If they were to have a chance of coming out of the encounter alive, he would have to use his wits—and his gun. That realization had a sobering effect on him, but he thrust it aside immediately. He and Jenny were facing death, and what had to be done, must be done.

He raised his eyes, looked beyond the men into the shadows of the stable's interior, and wondered where the hostler or the livery barn's owner might be. There was no sign of them. Evidently Monty had gotten rid of anyone that had been present when they arrived, perhaps locking them in the feed room or some other available

141

space.

"Nobody around if that's what you're hoping to see," Killeen said in a cold, level voice. "There's just you and me, Frank. I always wondered which one of us would walk away after shooting it out. You once were faster, but I figure I'm better than you now."

"Not hard to claim that when you've already got your gun out."

"And it's staying out," Killeen said coolly. "That's what makes me better than you. I think faster."

"You'll never be the man Frank is!" Jenny shouted, suddenly angered. "Not if you live to be a hundred!"

Monty laughed. "I'll give you the answer to that real soon."

"Come on, come on—let's get it done with," Vinson said impatiently, glancing around. "All this jawing and haggling, somebody'll be showing up here."

"You can look for that deputy and the marshal both to show up the minute there's shooting," Bratton said, again looking around. There was still no one in sight.

"Hell, that hayseed deputy won't give us no trouble. Augie'll take care of him. And that two-bit marshal, I expect he's sleeping his head off by now. I'm through talking. Toss me that money."

Frank Bratton tensed, steeled himself for what the next few moments would hold. Giving Jenny a side look, he smiled faintly and then, reaching back with his left hand, took up the pair of saddlebags, now empty, that had held the flatrock money.

"All yours, Monty," he said, and, throwing them with all his strength at Killeen, launched himself from the saddle.

In that same fragment of time he drew his gun and fired point-blank at Killeen—staggering back from the

142

impact of the heavy leather pouches striking him. Monty went hard against the edge of the stable's door frame. A shocked look covered his handsome face as he slowly began to sink.

But Frank Bratton saw none of that. He knew his bullet had gone true and he was now prone in the dust, rolling frantically to one side as he tried desperately to avoid the bullets that Augie Vinson was throwing at him. Beyond Vinson, Dollar Smith was rushing up, his weapon out and ready.

Frank checked his motion, reversed, paused, and triggered a shot at Vinson. The slim, dark man staggered, spun half-around. In that moment Bratton felt a slug drive into his leg, setting up a wave of pain while another burned across his arm as Smith opened up. Steadying himself, he fired at Dollar.

Abruptly more gunshots sounded, unaccountably, from the rear of the hotel. With both Vinson and Dollar Smith no longer visible before him in the haze of dust and smoke, Bratton twisted around. Harry Locke was running toward him.

As pain slogged through him Frank swore grimly. This would likely put an end to his chances of going free. Even if he was able to prove he was not guilty of anything at Charlie's Place, shooting down Killeen and his two partners would go against him. Any man with a prison record, one that noted previous killings, could kiss freedom and the future good-bye.

"Frank . . ."

Bratton drew himself to a sitting position, aware of Jenny kneeling beside him. He stared at her dully. "Reckon I've gone and done it for sure. Was never going to use my gun on a man again, long as I lived. Now I've shot down three."

143

"You didn't have a choice—you've got to realize that. If you hadn't killed them, they would have killed you." Jenny hesitated, looked up at Harry Locke standing quietly nearby. "I knew this was coming, and I was afraid—afraid Frank would get himself killed because he didn't want to use his gun."

"Sure didn't have no choice," the lawman said. "It was either use that iron or set there and get shot. Who are these men?"

Jenny, glancing around at the dozen or so bystanders looking on, ignored the lawman's question.

"Somebody, please—get the doctor!" she said.

"He's coming," a voice in the crowd replied.

His pain now a dull ache, Bratton checked the bleeding in his leg with a wadded bandanna, then turned his attention to Locke.

"They're the ones that held up the way station at Flatrock," he said, answering for Jenny. "They were after the money they took—and lost."

The marshal frowned. "How's it happen you know all about that? Was you in on it?"

"Hell, no, Marshal. You know that! I was on the run from you when that was going on. I just heard about it. It was those three, a couple more that got shot, and a . ."

Bratton paused, looked beyond the crumpled shape of Monty Killeen to the doorway where the girl, Becky, had been sitting. There was no sign of her. She had apparently slipped off unseen when the shooting was over. Let it go at that, he thought. Bringing the girl into it now would serve no good purpose.

"That's what I know about it."

Locke reloaded his six-gun and holstered it. The doctor, accompanied by Deputy Harden, trotted up, both sweating profusely. The physician hunched beside

Frank and began to examine the leg wound.

"Well, I sure don't see how you could've been mixed up in it," Locke commented idly. "Like you said, you was right busy running from me. I reckon it was the money you found that set them three jaspers after you."

"He could've kept right on going with that cash had he been of a mind," Harden said. "Nobody'd sure known the difference."

"For a fact," Locke said. "Reckon I've had you figured wrong all the time, Bratton, and I'm man enough to admit it. You can forget about Charlie's Place. I'll go down there and straighten it out myself."

Jenny came to her feet and whirled to face the lawman. "You mean he's free to go?"

"I reckon he is, soon as the doc fixes him up."

"Which won't take much," the physician said. "Only a flesh wound. Bullet went straight through. Leg's going to be a bit sore for a few days."

Bratton glanced at the medical man. "That mean I can't set a saddle?"

The physician, completing his bandaging, shrugged. "It would be painful."

Frank looked up at Jenny. "I reckon we'll be hanging around here for a spell before we head out for Denver or wherever." He paused, grinned. "And expect we best find that preacher we were talking about."

We hope that you enjoyed reading this
Sagebrush Large Print Western.
If you would like to read more Sagebrush titles,
ask your librarian or contact the Publishers:

United States and Canada

Thomas T. Beeler, *Publisher*
Post Office Box 659
Hampton Falls, New Hampshire 03844-0659
(800) 251-8726

United Kingdom, Eire, and
the Republic of South Africa

Isis Publishing Ltd
7 Centremead
Osney Mead
Oxford OX2 0ES England
(01865) 250333

Australia and New Zealand

Australian Large Print Audio & Video P/L
17 Mohr Street
Tullamarine, Victoria, 3043, Australia
1 800 335 364

Check Out Receipt

Newmarket Public Library

905-953-5110
www.newmarketpl.ca

Patron: POTGIETER, GERHARDUS
Date: 2018-09-04 2:21:21 PM

1. Apache Mountain justice
Barcode 35923000880301
Due by 2018-09-25 11:59 PM

2. Outlaw marshal
Barcode 35923002958777
Due by 2018-09-25 11:59 PM

3. The brass bullet
Barcode 35923000424574
Due by 2018-09-25 11:59 PM

4. Warpath
Barcode 35923000570863
Due by 2018-09-25 11:59 PM

Try Hoopla today!
1000s of movies and TV shows
you can stream.

Find it at
www.newmarketpl.ca/free
under eMusic